Romance Book Club

What really happens behind the scenes?

Michelle Hughes

Tears of Crimson Publishing

Tears of Crimson Publishing
Rockford, AL
www.tearsofcrimson.com

Publisher's Note: This is a work of fiction. Names, characters, places, and incidents are a product of the author's imagination. Locales and public names are sometimes used for atmospheric purposes. Any resemblance to actual people, living or dead, or to businesses, companies, events, institutions, or locales is completely coincidental.

Book Layout ©2013 BookDesignTemplates.com

Romance Book Club/ Michelle Hughes. -- 1st ed.
ISBN: 978-1484149218
LCN: 2013939443

Dedicated to a beautiful soul who gave me a love of romance reading from an early age. Your sweet smile and encouraging words are missed every single day, and I look forward to sharing all the things that have happened since you've taken your walk into peace when we meet again someday. Granny, if you're looking down I hope you can smile knowing the gift you gave lives on in me every day.

Acknowledgements

Thank you so much to the incredible friends who stood by my side as I took the time to create a new romantic adventure. Tammie Clarke Gibbs, SJ Byrne, Brandy Dorsch, and Camille Burgin without your support this book would have never seen the light of day. To my incredible mom, Susan, and my beautiful sisters, Angela and Rachel your unwavering love reminds me always of how important family is! To my husband Jay, and my beautiful children Jon, Kayla, Kaitlin, Jeremy and Jacob who don't read romance, but always give me their love; this one is for you. As always, thank you so much to the Friends of Crimson!

CHAPTER ONE

Sensation's

She didn't belong here. That was the thought that pummeled Jessie Lawrence's mind like an unwanted song lyric that got stuck in your head. All the leather, and deviant acts of pleasure being enacted around her were so far removed from her life, it didn't even make sense that she'd been invited in.

But here she was, her name on a contract stating she wouldn't reveal what went on inside Sensation's Dungeon, sitting across from one of the sexiest men she'd seen outside the movies. She listened to Chase Davenport casually describe the lifestyle of a master and submissive, as if it were an everyday conversation topic. That kind of talk was almost as unfamiliar to her as the urge to reach up and see if that five o'clock shadow on his face was as rough as it looked.

She'd balked earlier when they'd visited the main dungeon playroom after seeing acts that, in her mind, were so depraved, no person should ever consent to them. That was how she found herself separated from the group she'd arrived with and listening to the owner of the club as he tried to convince her there was more to this lifestyle than what she'd witnessed earlier.

"Would you like to visit one of the private rooms so you can put a visual to the scenarios I'm describing? I promise it won't be as overwhelming as seeing all those scenes taking place at the same time."

What was he talking about? Biting her lip nervously, she nodded, hoping that was the right response, since she'd stopped hearing his words somewhere around the point at which he explained the pleasures a submissive might feel when having her hands bound.

Standing up to his full six foot four inch height, he smiled down on her. "I think you'll understand a little more if I demonstrate the way we use some of the toys at our disposal."

Jessie gave a small smile, and another nod. This all started with her romance book club. At the moment she was regretting letting her best friend Amanda talk her into joining that group of women. They had a little too much curiosity to understand that everything they read about didn't need to be explored. With her stomach quivering nervously, she attempted to keep up with Chase's long strides.

She tried never to judge people by their looks, but even she couldn't help but notice how fine his jeans enhanced his well-formed backside. She suddenly found herself wondering how it would feel to have her hands grip said backside as he brought her body to heights of pleasure she'd yet to experience.

Maybe laying off the steamy romance books was a good idea? Why else, after all these years of self-denial, was her libido deciding to kick in? Entering the room that looked more like an ancient torture chamber than a place where a person discovered pleasure, she took a step back and let out her breath quickly.

He heard her gasp and turned to face her. "These objects can't hurt you, they're just wood, leather, and chains." Smiling reassuringly, he waited for her to join him.

Drawn by the sensual timbre of his voice, she entered the room. The strange cross in the back corner caught her attention. Letting her curiosity lead her, she found herself in front of it, her hand running over the smooth wood.

The polished wood led up to embedded chains at the top. Dangling, angry looking leather cuffs drifted from the links. What would it feel like, she wondered, to be bound helplessly to this contraption without any way to escape? She shivered, and then turned her eyes back to the gorgeous man giving her the tour.

He obviously noted her interest and gave a satisfied grin. "Why don't you strap me in so you can see what it looks like in use?"

She quickly shook her head no. Strangely, the thought of this beautiful man trapped helplessly in the device had her body aching with something she wasn't ready to put a name to. *It has to be the place*, she thought. Closing her eyes, she took a deep breath. She couldn't really want to explore the actions he was suggesting.

"Maybe you'd prefer allowing me to control you this way instead?" Smirking, he motioned with his hand for her to step toward the cross.

"No!" Flushing, she lowered her tone before speaking again. "I just have no idea how to attach you to this thing." Jessie's heart was racing, and disgust was the furthest thing from her mind. She wanted to experience what it felt like to be completely helpless, and that terrified her beyond belief.

"Don't worry. I'll walk you through it," Chase said, moving to position his body on the cross. He chuckled softly. "Just buckle me in with the wrist restraints."

Awkwardly she buckled his strong hands into the contraption. Thankful for the small step-ladder that stood on each side of the expansive contraption, she had no problem reaching his wrists. He was almost completely immobile now, and that forced a small sigh from her lips. Shifting her weight from one foot to the other, she attempted to control the desire that had her clenching the muscles in her thighs. "What next?" She whispered the words, afraid he would know how the sight of him bound this way was turning her on.

He struggled, and Jessie knew it was for her benefit to show that he couldn't release himself without help. "Look down at my feet. There are two ankle restraints there. Do the same thing."

This shouldn't be so sexy, was what repeated in her head. She was almost panting at the delicious thoughts moving through her mind, and she had barely even touched him. Unconsciously, her hand moved up his covered leg as she stood. She needed to have more contact.

He waited for her to stand before speaking again. "It's a strange sensation being on the receiving end for a change."

"I guess this is what your women feel like?" Taking a step back, she hesitantly allowed her eyes to roam over him.

"I don't have women, per sé. I choose to do this with a partner." Stretching his arms in the shackles, he shrugged. "At the moment, I'm single."

"I admit I'm amazed you don't play around." Flushing, she stammered out, "What I meant was, I'm sure women are throwing themselves at ..." Stopping mid-sentence, she realized her words told him exactly how attractive she found him.

"Thank you, I think," He smiled at the compliment. "So you find me irresistible, huh?"

She could tell he knew just how attractive he was. "Incorrigible, perhaps." Grinning and rolling her eyes she decided to toy with him a little. "So I have you all tied up and completely at my mercy." The statement made her heart race and she couldn't resist studying his incredible physique. Even fully clothed in jeans and a dark t-shirt that accentuated his perfect body, he was unbelievably seductive.

"If the situation was reversed, I'd have you begging by now."

Catching her breath at his words and the smirk on his face, Jessie wet her lips without thought. "I should let you go." *In more ways than one.* He was obviously experienced in the game of seduction and she was no match for a man like him. Even if he made her mind ache to explore the possibilities, she was basically working without a script. Not giving him time to argue, she moved to the ankle cuffs, releasing them before unbinding his hands.

"Shame." Glancing over her wickedly, he patiently smiled. "Would you like to explore the rest of the room?"

"I'm sure the other ladies are wondering if I left. I should probably get back with my group." *Before you do something idiotic,* she chided herself as she schooled her expression into one that said it had been fun but the games were over.

"If you're sure?" He forced a small smile.

"I've monopolized enough of your time and I'm sure that's not what you were looking forward to when Carolyn invited us here tonight." It was Carolyn's confession of living this lifestyle, combined with the BDSM themed book they were reading this month that had brought them here.

"To be honest, I'm glad Carolyn invited your group, especially you."

She didn't know how to react to his compliment and decided to change the subject, hoping her face wasn't bright red. "How did you get in to all this. I mean, you seem like such a normal guy?" *Mouth filter Jessie,* she reprimanded herself.

"I had a girlfriend in college who enjoyed bondage, and after she moved on I decided to discover more." Shrugging his shoulders, he added, "That was over ten years ago and I just kept experimenting until I found out what worked for me."

"So no abusive background or a need to degrade women?" She was confused. The romance book characters always seemed to have some horrible past. She'd just assumed that was normal for people in this type of lifestyle.

Chuckling, he shook his head. "My father is a great man. As far as woman go, I happen to love them, and consider myself a man that enjoys pleasing not degrading."

"Huh. That doesn't really fit in with the alpha male thing we're reading about."

"I don't read romance, but I doubt much of what you read in a fictional story has a basis in reality. I've seen many women in the last year finding their way into my club because of some book." Chase grinned, shaking his head.

"I have to say you're nothing like those men I've read about, which isn't a bad thing." She'd come here tonight half-expecting to see men who dragged women around by their hair. Instead she'd met this man, who was anything but rude.

"I have my moments. So you haven't run out the door screaming yet. Should I take that to mean you're still interested in learning more?"

His unabashed grin, made her wonder what he was thinking. She nodded her head, a little surprised. She realized she was actually enjoying herself. "Actually, this has been more educational than I thought. You don't seem like the type of man to drag an unwilling woman into your arms." She wasn't even sure anymore if she'd be unwilling, if it came to that. Her face flushed hotly.

Chase chuckled. "I'm glad your opinion of me is so high. To be honest, I'm enjoying your company." Taking her elbow in his hand, he gave it a gentle squeeze. "We'll venture out into the main area again, but if you feel uncomfortable, just let me know and I'll get you out of there immediately."

A part of her didn't want to join the others again. There was no way she could tell this virile man that. With a small smile, she nodded and allowed him to lead her away from the temptation being alone with him presented. Reminding herself that he was a stranger and that casual sex was definitely not her thing, helped ease the disappointment her body felt at not giving in to the temptation.

The main room was still overwhelming. There were so many different scenes taking places in varying corners. The cross he'd introduced her to in the other room had a shirtless woman attached to it here and she was being flogged by someone Jessie assumed was her master. The woman seemed to be enjoying the punishment, judging from the soft moans pouring from her lips. The sounds of pleasure resonated within her and she was shocked to realize she was a little jealous she wasn't experiencing the sensation.

On another side of the room, a heavy set male was being paddled on the spanking bench, and the site of his bare ass was a little more than she was interested in seeing, so she turned away with a flush coloring her cheeks. Her senses were overloaded and it was hard to know where to rest her eyes. Some strange bars caught her attention. They were being put to use by a couple whose actions made her cringe. Each sound of a hollow cane falling on the woman's bare ass made her shiver.

"Caning is something that you need to work up to." Apparently noting her discomfort, Chase steered her away from the play. "I see your friends are enjoying a piercing demonstration. Maybe we should join them?"

She nodded nervously, and he smiled encouragingly before leading her over to the crowd of people watching the scene. "This is something I don't really enjoy, but it fascinates more than a few of the club members."

She wasn't sure if she was horrified or intrigued as she watched the man having small needles inserted into his back, just under the skin. She'd never seen anything like this in her life, and she couldn't deny she was somewhat curious. When the ends of those needles were lit on fire, she'd seen enough, and turned back to Chase. "That's definitely something that doesn't appeal to me," she whispered into his ear, after standing on tip toes to reach it.

"So does anything else appeal to you here?" He waited for her to answer patiently.

"Well, the flogging maybe. The sounds of the woman over there tell me she's really enjoying it." Glancing at her feet, realizing what she admitted, her face burned.

"Flogging can be very sensual. I could demonstrate for you if you're interested." Chase smiled warmly.

"I'm still not sure I could do that though. I mean, it's a lot to think about. What I mean is..," She trailed off not sure why she was suddenly so nervous, but even her hands were shaking.

"Relax. I'm not asking you to make a decision now. I'm just saying that the door is open for you if you ever choose to walk through." Pulling out a business card from his pocket listing his name and the clubs, he took out a pen and wrote his cell phone number on the back. "If you ever decide you want to explore, give me a call. Or if you'd just like to talk some more about this. I've really enjoyed having you here tonight."

She was truly flattered, and overwhelmed that this handsome man was interested in teaching her more, but even so, she didn't think she could accept the offer. "I really appreciate it, Chase. If I ever decide to consider this, you'll be the first person I call." That was definitely the truth, she thought, because she didn't know anyone besides Carolyn, who was into this kind of thing.

"I hope you do, Jessie, and if not, maybe you'll just allow me to take you to dinner one night. You have my number. Just let me know." With a smile, he guided her back to her friends, who had moved on to witness a knife play scene.

"Ladies, thank you for joining us tonight. Carolyn, your friends are welcome here any time." He gave them all a smile before turning to Jessie and winking. "Hope to talk to you soon."

"Wow, what was that all about?" Amanda turned away from the erotic knife play scene to stare at her.

Attempting not to watch Chase as he walked away, Jessie shrugged. "The owner was just worried I'd gotten the wrong idea about his club, and offered to talk with me again if I was interested sometime." There was no way she was adding any more than that.

"If you're interested, talk to Carolyn about him. Apparently they've been friends for years and she should know if he's trustworthy." Amanda looked surprised at the idea that Jessie would even consider talking to the owner.

Shaking her head, Jessie gave a half-hearted smile. "The man was just being nice. I'm not the type who could enjoy something like this." The lie felt cheap as it left her lips. She was more interested in Chase than she'd ever been in a man since Greg.

Shrugging her shoulders, Amanda nodded. "Even I might have problems with some of these things." She turned her attention back to the knife play.

Regardless of her interest, she was going to put him out of her mind the minute she walked out the door. The man was definitely handsome, and without doubt charming, so yes he intrigued her. She would be crazy to even consider the possibility of becoming involved with a man like Chase. Maybe if he wasn't into all the kinky stuff. No, she definitely was putting the thought to bed. *A bed with him in it,* her thoughts wandered. "Definitely not interested." *Liar,* her subconscious chided.

It wasn't a big secret, at least between Jessie and Amanda, that Jessie was sexually repressed. Her idea of a hot night of lovemaking was reading a sexy book and falling asleep to dream about it. She didn't date, and had turned down several attempts to set her up. She had her job, her cats, and her books. What more could a woman want?

They watched various other scenes play out for the next hour before Carolyn asked to be driven home. She explained that she had early appointments, and the rest of the group decided without her there, they didn't feel very comfortable in staying.

Jessie wished she'd at least caught another glimpse of Chase before she left, but he was nowhere to be seen.

As they walked out the door, she decided it was probably for the best. She didn't belong in his world.

Resting in her bed later that night, her favorite companion Sebastian purring as he slept on her chest, she rethought the evening. Rubbing the soft fur behind his ears, she smiled in contentment. This was a safe life, and didn't involve having her emotions ripped to shreds or leaving her heart shattered because she dared to trust another human being.

Closing her eyes, Chase Davenport's beautiful face filled her mind. It wasn't worth it. No man as sexy as him could ever be satisfied with a wallflower like her. Forcing her eyes to open, she glanced into Sebastian's feline eyes. "You'd never let me down, would you, baby?" Smiling at his responding purr, she put all thoughts of the handsome stranger out of her head.

CHAPTER TWO

Reminiscing

Knowing what was right didn't always mean your mind would get on the same page. During the next four nights, all her dreams were filled with Chase in one scenario or another. They were usually at the club when her fantasy started, but on a few nights she imagined them rolling in red silk sheets on what she imagined was his bed, since her own sported practical white linens.

Working from home was the only reason she hadn't gotten behind on her assignments. Her mind just couldn't focus. Having her thoughts disturbed not only in dreams, but at many points during the day by a half-naked, gorgeous hunk was taking a toll. Fixing Sebastian his favorite bowl of kitty chow in the kitchen, she shook her head in disgust at her mental debauchery.

The book club was meeting tonight, and she hadn't even read the featured novel because every time she started to read, her mind went off into fantasy land. Obviously her body wasn't happy with the way she'd been denying her needs. She could never give in to Amanda's idea and purchase a battery operated boyfriend. She had nothing against sex toys, but the thought of using them on her own body wasn't appealing.

She considered bailing on the group tonight, but Amanda was hosting. Not showing up would hurt her friend's feelings, and she knew there was a guest speaker planned. If there was one thing you didn't miss, it was a night with a speaker. Usually they were authors', and it took considerable planning to arrange their visits.

With a sigh, she stepped into the shower, knowing she wasn't going to play hooky. They were still discussing that BDSM story and she knew it would remind her of Chase, but even that wasn't enough to make her risk upsetting her best friend. She wished the steaming mist would help her relax instead of make her imagine the feel of a certain sexy man's hands all over her body.

Frustrated, she stepped out and wrapped herself in an oversized bath towel. Three years without a date was ridiculous. Maybe she *should* consider letting Amanda set her up with someone. Maybe a sexy dungeon owner who enjoyed tying women up? Shaking her head, she quickly dismissed that thought. Some nice man, who wasn't complicated, made much more sense.

Her thoughts turned to the reason she'd stopped dating as she wiped away the condensation on the bathroom mirror. Greg Foster. The first year without Greg, she'd considered herself in mourning, and had shut herself off from the rest of the world. He'd broken her heart in ways that couldn't be easily forgotten, even if he wasn't at fault for finally realizing he wasn't into women.

He'd been her first love and they'd dated since tenth grade in high school. Back in those days, she hadn't thought much of him not being interested in sex. In many ways, it had been a blessing not to have to deal with all the drama of teenage sex.

They'd decided to go to college together, still a couple, and he was a hugely attentive boyfriend compared to those of her peers. He always complimented her on her looks, and took her to events most young men would have balked at. But as a freshman in college, surrounded by people enjoying their own sexuality, her sudden new need to explore became more of a craving.

Greg had tried to be what she needed, but the awkward petting was never very satisfying for either of them. Maybe in hindsight she'd known he was gay, because when he touched her it was just embarrassing or felt plain wrong. The end of their freshman year, he'd confessed he had feelings for another male student and for a while, her world had completely folded in on her.

When she was past the heartache, she realized they had bonded for life, and she'd offered him as much support as she could when he came out. She never admitted to him how much their breakup had damaged her own self-esteem, nor the fact that back then, she'd blamed herself for not being enough woman to satisfy him. And bizarrely, sometimes still felt that way.

They'd remained friends during her sophomore year of college, but after he met Barry, the love of his life, they slowly drifted apart. By the time graduation came, they barely spoke. Her goal in life became business, and if Amanda hadn't befriended her, she was pretty sure living out the rest of her life as a recluse would have been her fate.

Meeting Amanda had been one of those lucky deals, and she remembered to the day how it had come to be. She was working as an intern for the multi-billion dollar computer firm Amanda's father owned and had been called to service some software in her office.

Soon, she learned Amanda had no understanding of technology and it didn't seem to like her very much, either. Anytime she touched one of the desktops it seemed to malfunction. After Jessie's first month of working for Amanda's father, they were on a first name basis. She spent hour's computer coaching her new friend.

After a few more months, Amanda began inviting her to lunch every day, and their friendship continued to bloom. They were from two different worlds. While Jessie had struggled to pay for college by working side jobs, Amanda had everything she ever wanted handed to her on a silver platter. But even with all their differences, there was a bond that continued to grow between them. They complimented each other perfectly.

Slipping on a comfortable pair of jeans and a t-shirt, Jessie continued to mentally reminisce. She couldn't imagine not having Amanda in her life. With the death of her mother last year, Amanda was the only person she had to turn to. She had never known her father, and all her mother's family was half-way across the country.

Her friend had helped her get the work from home position with her father's business when it was listed. The depression she'd suffered after losing her mom had almost destroyed her. She'd barely been able to make it out of bed each morning, and had she not been given that job, she would probably have ended up living in poverty, as her mother had.

Greg's reveal had nothing on the devastation of knowing her mom had lost her life because she hadn't been able to fight her heroin addiction. She'd always struggled with the addiction but had managed to still be a parent in her own way. One half-way house to another had become her mother's fate after Jessie moved to campus, and she still blamed herself for not being at home to help her.

The depressing thoughts all crashed in on her now, and she knew going to the book club was the only practical means of escape. She couldn't change what her life had become, and considering her past, she felt fortunate that she had as normal a life as she did. Reaching down to stroke Sebastian, she forced a smile. "I'll be back home soon, baby."

CHAPTER THREE

Book Club

She made it to the book club, amazed her memories of Greg and her mother hadn't caused her to be later than she was. Walking through the door of Amanda's impressive condominium, she struggled to get her thoughts in order. Since meeting Chase it seemed all the bad memories had decided to haunt her at once. She'd almost believed she was at the point of finally starting to heal. Obviously her mind wasn't ready to let go of the pain.

Smoothing back a few stray hairs that escaped her ponytail, she wished she'd taken more time with her appearance. Confidence wasn't really her thing, and the women here were all polished. They all seemed friendly, but Jessie felt out of place.

Her jaw almost hit the floor when she saw who the guest speaker was as she entered the living room. Having all eyes turn toward her didn't help at all. She felt herself flush and hurriedly made her way to one of the oversized chairs, shooting Amanda a look. It took a few seconds to calm her racing heart as she sat down in the last free chair.

"Glad you could join us Jessie. Carolyn invited me over to talk with the group about the romance aspect of BDSM, since it's a topic you're reading about this month." Chase smiled warmly.

"Nice to see you again, Chase," she whispered a greeting as she pulled the book out of her purse and focused her attention on it. She couldn't imagine sitting here for an entire hour listening to him speak after the fantasies she'd had of him this week. Hoping her face wasn't as red as it felt, she fought back a wave of nerves.

"So one of the things Carolyn has explained to me, is that most of the male dominants in your books are egotistical and almost abusive. Let me assure you that in the real world of this lifestyle, that's not normally the case. We respect our submissive's. That type of mentality is something I would never support."

"A submissive is to be cherished for the gift of submission, and it's an honor to know she trusts you enough to put her well-being into your hands. People from the outside usually pay more attention to the tools or toys we use, but rarely take the time to understand the devotion behind the relationship itself. Above everything else, our relationships are safe, sane and consensual, and that's a motto every self-respecting dominant or submissive lives by."

"So how did you discover this lifestyle, if you don't mind me asking?" Lauren was one of the older women in the group, and Jessie was surprised she was interested in the topic.

"I had a girlfriend who introduced bondage to me in college. I was living in Chicago at the time. After experimenting a little with rope bondage, she invited me to a munch, which is another word for a meeting, and I was intrigued. After we parted ways, I remained connected with the group that hosted the munch's. Through that group I befriended a wonderful dominatrix who had been living the lifestyle for over forty years. We began talking and she helped me find my path."

"A dominatrix, isn't that a woman that beats men?" Amanda was obviously curious.

"I can answer that one, Chase." Carolyn smiled patiently. "We prefer to call what we do fulfilling the disciplinary needs of our submissive's, Amanda. For me, personally, the men that I play with enjoy pain and want a strong woman that is willing to humiliate them."

"I'm a little confused, Chase never mentioned humiliation." Jessie whispered, keeping her eyes focused on the book, shocked that the words had slipped from her mouth.

"Very astute, Jessie," Chase said, smiling at her question. "Carolyn and I have very different styles of playing. I consider myself more into the aspect of a loving master role, while Carolyn appreciates sadomasochism."

The conversation continued, and Jessie fought to keep her eyes off the gorgeous man talking. The questions were as diverse as the people in the room and secretly she was enjoying the discussion. When Chase stopped speaking, she discovered she missed the sound of his voice, and looked up. Finding his dark blue eyes staring straight into hers forced her to catch her breath.

Pulling her attention away, she realized they hadn't even discussed the book they'd read this week. She was somewhat grateful, having not read more than a few pages. Carolyn said they would go over the book next week, almost reading her thoughts. That gave her a week to catch up.

Chase walked over and reached down to pluck the book off Jessie's lap. Staring at the cover, he grinned then raised an eyebrow. "Pretty steamy pair."

"Um, yeah, I guess so," she said, fumbling over the words like an awkward teenager.

"So what do you get out of reading these books? I'm curious why women read these when they could explore with a partner instead."

"I can't speak for all women." God, her voice was trembling. This man was definitely not the type she should be interested in. He made her feel entirely too much.

"What about you, personally?" Lowering down to a knee so they could be on eye level, he rested his chin on his fist as he waited for her to answer.

The scent of his cologne wafted under her nostrils and she felt her mouth water. *Think, Jessie.* Her heart raced as she tried to consider his words and not the stunning man gazing into her eyes with an expression that left her longing. "I guess I like to imagine what they feel."

"Wouldn't it be more exciting to experience what they feel?" His eyes searched her face.

"It's safer to read about it," she admitted, her ability to think slowly disintegrating as she lost herself in his stare.

Chuckling softly, he stood up, still staring down into her eyes. "Perhaps safer, but not as memorable." Holding out his hand, he helped her stand.

Swallowing repeatedly, she couldn't deny the jolt of pleasure his warm hand combined with his words forced her to feel. She lowered her eyes. The intensity revealed in his gaze left her knees shaking. "Maybe." The soft-spoken words came out as a squeak and she felt awkward and confused.

"Feel like getting out of here and going for coffee?" Chase winked.

There were a dozen reasons why she should have said no, but she decided honesty was the way wanted to go. "I could handle some." Perhaps she should have chosen a better phrase. The wicked smile on his face made her think he thought she was discussing more than a drink.

"Same here." His smile broadened. "Do you need to tell your friend's goodnight before we leave?"

"I do." She smiled shyly. "I'll be right back." Shakiness was probably another sign she should make up an excuse not to go, but it was only coffee, she reasoned, not another trip to his dungeon. Making her way to Amanda, she hugged her. "Thanks for a fun evening."

"Are you leaving already? I thought a few of us could crack open some wine after the rest of the group leaves."

"Chase invited me for coffee, and I said yes." She lowered her eyes at her admission, not sure what her friend would think about her leaving with someone like him.

"Carolyn tells me he's a really nice guy," Amanda said, nodding. "I don't see what having coffee could hurt. I'll call you in an hour, just to make sure you made it home."

"That sounds good. Are we still on for lunch tomorrow?"

"Absolutely. There's a new Italian restaurant that opens tomorrow and I'm dying to try it out." After giving her friend another brief hug, she glanced at her intently. "Take care."

"I will, and I'll see you around noon?" She wasn't really worried about Chase trying anything.

"Sounds good. Have fun." She waved Jessie off with a smile.

Jessie's nervousness increased as she and Chase made their way down to his sleek sports car. Then, she realized the feeling was anticipation, not nervousness. She was very aware of him as a man, more so than she'd ever been with Greg and the feeling was new to her. It had been a long time since she'd allowed herself to think of a man as anything other than a business contact.

"There's a great little coffee shop on Marietta Street, unless you'd like to go somewhere else?" Turning his eyes to her, his brow furrowed.

For a dominant male, he didn't seem pushy at all. "Whatever you think is fine with me," she said. Focusing on her clenched hands in her lap, she just hoped she didn't stumble through a conversation with him.

"Charged words, Jessie, and every dom's dream." He chuckled softly, "You can relax, I promise not to go all alpha male on you tonight."

Unclenching her hands, she shrugged apologetically. "I trust you." She kept quiet after that comment, until they parked outside the coffee house. Afraid that anything that came out of her mouth would be misinterpreted. He guided her inside, his hand at the middle of her back, and she was more than aware of it the entire time.

The place was thankfully not overcrowded, which was unusual except for this time of night during the week. Finding an empty table away from the few people who were there was easy, and he led her to it, even holding her chair out. "They have great cakes here, if you're interested?"

"Just a coffee for me please. I have to keep up my girlish figure." She laughed self-consciously and tried to remember the last time she'd actually been on a date.

"I think you look perfect." With a wink to her, he waved the waitress over.

They ordered their drinks and he filled up what would have been awkward silence with conversation on normal topics. He listened intently as she discussed her job. Jessie couldn't remember the last time anyone had acted this interested in her.

"So what about you?" She was curious about the man behind the club. "Outside of the club, do you have hobbies?"

"I have many actually, I love to skydive, hike, go to concerts, and even though I'm not a big romance reader, I enjoy reading biographies of famous people." He stopped to take a breath.

"Wow, those first few hobbies make you sound like quite the adventurer. I can't say I've done much of that sort of thing." She was more an indoor type of person, but the thought of doing some of those things with another person didn't sound half bad.

"Maybe you'll let me take you some time. Perhaps we could start with a hike. Being surrounded by nature is something everyone should experience."

"I think I'd like that, as long as we're not talking mountain climbing. I'm not sure I have the endurance for that." She tried to go running a few times a week, it helped clear her head when a project was stressing her out, but she didn't consider herself a health nut, by any means.

"We'd have to work up to the mountain climbing," he said, grinning. "That's not something you can just jump straight into."

"Speaking of that," she got his reference immediately, "do you ever have relationships that don't involve that lifestyle?" That was the real question here for her.

He seemed like an incredible man, and he was obviously very educated, but she was just an average girl.

"It's part of who I am, Jessie." He smiled and took a sip of his coffee, seeming to gauge her reaction.

It was hard to hide her disappointment. The truth was, he was the first man since Greg she had an interest in, but the baggage he came with, well, it was a lot to consider.

He shrugged apologetically and took another sip of his coffee.

"I'll be honest with you, Chase. Me and sexuality," she paused as she glanced at her coffee cup so as not to meet his eyes, "they don't exactly mesh." They didn't even live on the same planet, as far as she was concerned. After Greg she'd suppressed all her sexual needs and kept them in a place in her mind that had a No Entry sign until recently.

"I find that hard to believe Jessie. You're a beautiful woman, and obviously very intelligent, so why would you not explore your sensual nature?" Perplexed, he studied her face.

"It's a really long story." Laughing nervously, she lifted her cup and took a small sip.

"I have all the time in the world, unless you'd rather not share?" Chase raised an eyebrow. "I admit it Jessie, I'm curious about you."

She concentrated on her drink for a few minutes as she tried to decide how much she was willing to reveal to this man. "If you really want to know, I guess I don't mind sharing." It wasn't a huge secret, even though she'd only shared it with Amanda.

"I do. Would you like to go to one of my favorite spots to talk about it? The coffee shop will be closing soon. I promise I'm not taking you back to my dungeon." He grinned at her nod. Walking to the counter, he settled the bill and ordered them two cups to go.

Amanda called as she arrived at the car, and she was a little amazed an hour had already passed. She quickly told her everything was fine, and promised to meet her for lunch. She enjoyed the companionable silence as Chase drove her to their destination.

She was surprised when they arrived on top of Lookout Mountain. It was one of her favorite views of the city below and a place she visited a few times. "I love this place," she smiled as they got out of the car.

"Same here. There's something incredible about looking over the city but being away from it at the same time. Give me a moment and I'll grab us a blanket." Moving to his trunk, he released the latch and pulled it out.

She laughed softly at his preparedness. "So do you always carry a blanket around in your trunk?" She should probably be offended, she thought, but somehow she couldn't be.

"I carry blankets, bottled water, and medical supplies all the time. On hikes, you never know what you might need." They spread the blanket together and sat down. "So tell me the story of your life, Jessie." He leaned back on his muscular arms and waited for her to begin.

"You surprise me Chase," she felt guilty for jumping to conclusions. He didn't seem concerned so she followed his lead. Leaning back on her elbows, she looked up at the night stars. She wasn't sure how to tell the story, so she began at when she and Greg first starting dating in high school. Walking him through the years of their relationship, she realized her heart no longer ached at losing him. She left it at her mother's battle with the addiction that finally claimed her life.

"About Greg," he said, "The breakup was probably hard on both of you."

"It was. He was really a nice man, and I know he couldn't change who he was. I only wish he'd discovered his homosexuality earlier in life."

"None of us can change what we long for, Jessie." Reaching up, he pulled a strand of hair away from her eyes and smiled warmly.

It was definitely to his credit that he had such an open mind. She had never encountered homosexuality before Greg, but she believed every person had the right to make his or her own decisions. "I know Greg never felt comfortable with me as a woman."

"It wasn't you, Jessie. I hope you understand that. He was gay, and there was nothing you or any other woman could have done to change that fact."

"I guess I do still worry it was something I couldn't give him that made him turn out that way." She'd never admitted that to another living soul, and saying it out loud was truly freeing.

"Jessie, how long have you been carrying that around? Trust me, it was nothing you did or didn't do. It was who he was. You're a beautiful woman, and until you understand that about your relationship with him, it will be impossible to move forward."

For the first time in her life, she wanted to believe it wasn't her fault. Maybe it was the moonlight, or the fact that she was lying on a blanket with a gorgeous hunk of a man. Or maybe she finally realized she knew, somewhere deep in her subconscious, that she didn't have that much power over any person's decisions. Whatever it was, it felt like a weight lifted from her shoulders.

"It's been a long night. I should probably get you home so you can rest."

She was disappointed that he wanted to call an end to the night, and worried that she might have offended him. "I hope I didn't say something wrong," she nibbled her lower lip nervously.

"Jessie, I'm trying to be a gentleman here, I would love nothing more than to make passionate love to you and share every facet of my lifestyle. I'm only a man though, so unless that's what you want, you need to let me do the right thing here."

To say she was stunned would be putting it mildly, over his confession. To say it didn't turn her on immediately would be nothing but a blatant lie. The look of desire that filled his dark blue eyes made her ache with need, and knowing it was her he was looking at that way, in her opinion was nothing short of a miracle. "So what's stopping you?" She whispered, shocked at her ability to be so forward.

"Jessie I'm not a man who plays games," he warned her. "If you are willing to try this, then you need to be absolutely certain it's what you want, I couldn't live with myself if you regretted this later

"I don't know much about your world Chase, but I feel something for you that I don't want to walk away from." She felt she had to be honest with him. It was crazy to hope that they had any chance at a relationship, they barely knew each other, but there was a part of her willing to at least try.

"I know enough for both of us Jess," he chuckled warmly, "but I need you to go home tonight and think about what you're willing to do here. I understand the lifestyle is somewhat foreign to you, but I can walk you through that with patience and time. What I don't want is for you to make a hasty decision. We've had a good time together tonight, and you've revealed some very personal things in your life, so it could all be just a release from that part of your life."

She found it somewhat amusing that he seemed to be encouraging her to change her mind, and wondered if she shouldn't take his advice. Was she really willing to explore her sensuality in such a way with him? She was an intelligent woman and understood this wouldn't be just a dating relationship if she agreed. He'd already admitted who he was, so she couldn't pretend to not know what he would offer her.

"Let me take you home, and you can call me tomorrow if you decide this is something you want to pursue. If you don't then there won't be any hard feelings, but if you do then I'll expect you to a least give me a solid chance to share my world with you."

She nodded, even though her libido definitely wanted to explore something with him now that had little to do with talking. She'd pushed that part of her mentality back years ago, so a few more hours didn't make much of a difference. Helping him fold the blanket, they got back in the car for the short drive back to Amanda's where she left her car. "What do mean by a solid chance Chase, I want to understand what I'm thinking about tonight?"

They pulled up to Carolyn's condo as he turned to face her. "Give me a month at least Jessie, after that you can make an informed decision. After that you'll know if this is a lifestyle for you, and if you want to continue having me train and mentor or even have a relationship." Sliding out of the car he walked over to her side and opened the door.

He'd definitely given her something to think about, a month with him teaching her, that was probably the most exciting offer she was ever going to get in her lifetime, she thought. He walked her to her car and checked the backseat before opening her car door.

"I had a really good time tonight Jessie."

Last week she'd decided that never seeing him again was a smart idea, tonight she'd offered to give in to anything he wanted. She needed to sit down alone and decide just what she truly wanted. "I enjoyed being with you tonight Chase," feeling a little overwhelmed at the strange thoughts moving through her mind, she needed to escape and just take a little time to get her thoughts together.

"Drive carefully," he dropped a small kiss on her cheek and she smiled absently before watching him walk back to his car.

He backed out his car, since he was blocking her in, and she pulled out. Driving back home she wondered if she'd lost her mind. She'd divulged her life story to a man that was basically a stranger. Not to mention that she'd offered to warm his bed. Chase Davenport was dangerous to her idea of self-preservation, she decided. *Do you really want to keep playing it safe?*

CHAPTER FOUR

Friendship

She hadn't slept much, and now that it was morning, she, knew she had to come to a decision. Chase had been more than incredible last night, not taking advantage of her emotional state after they'd discussed her past. She doubted many men would have been that respectful. It said a lot about his character.

Jessie's dreams had been filled with him and oddly enough, they had little to do with the things he'd shown her in the dungeon. In her fantasy they were climbing a mountain, and when they reached the top, he wrapped her in his arms and then leisurely made love to her with only the sky witnessing their passion.

It was a beautiful dream and when the alarm clock woke her up, she wanted to toss it against the wall.

Attempting to wipe the sleep out of her eyes, she noted it was an hour before noon. It took her several minutes to remember she had a lunch date with Amanda. Her week was definitely proving to be interesting, for a change. Showering quickly, she felt a little more alive, but still, she would have enjoyed another three hours of rest.

Drying her hair quickly, she applied a pink gloss to her lips and a little mascara. Downtown Atlanta was always busy during lunch hour, so she knew she didn't have a lot of time to waste if she was going to be on time. After sliding on a casual dress, and her sandals, she grabbed her purse off the nightstand, and hurried out the door.

Parking was insane but finally she found a spot that had her walking only two blocks to the new restaurant. Amanda was waiting outside and she waved to catch her attention. Catching up to her, Jessie quickly apologized. "I didn't get much sleep last night," she offered weakly.

"You've been having a lot of trouble this week with sleep, Jessie. Are you getting sick?"

"Just preoccupied." Jessie wanted to wait until they were sitting down to talk about Chase. She knew if anyone knew her, it was Amanda. Maybe she could help her make sense of the strange feelings she was experiencing.

"You'll have to tell me about it," Amanda said. "I made a reservation, so let's order our lunch and chat."

They entered the quaint, but stylish restaurant and Jessie was impressed. From the outside the place didn't look like much, but in here the Italianate decor was lovely. They both ordered and waited for the waitress to walk away before trying to talk.

"So talk to me, Jessie. What's got your mind tied up?"

"Chase asked me to consider dating him." That was probably the only term to describe what they would be doing if she accepted, but she wasn't entirely sure it was fitting.

"As in none of the kinky stuff and just two people going out?"

Jessie paused. "More like him teaching me some of his kinky stuff and going out," she said finally.

"Wow. J, just... wow," Amanda sat back in stunned silence.

She wanted Amanda's approval. They were more like family than friends. What she thought mattered. "That's not much help Amanda," Jessie grinned, thinking it was usually Amanda who shocked her, not vice versa.

"What can I say, Jessie. I'm floored here. Steamy romance novels are one thing, but to experience a real life BDSM relationship?" Amanda lowered her voice to a whisper, "I think maybe you should talk to Carolyn before you make any kind of decision."

"I like Carolyn, Amanda, but we don't really talk outside of book club. It would be more awkward talking about this with her." Her introverted nature made it hard to get close to people, and the only one of that group she felt truly comfortable with was Amanda.

"You should really give her a chance. I know she really likes you and thinks you don't like her much. You really need to work on giving people a chance."

"I had no clue she felt that way. You know me, Amanda. I just don't do well with most people since Greg." All the other women at the book club seemed to have their act together, and she envied them for their ability to be so comfortable in their own skins.

"I know, and I told her it was nothing personal. Maybe this whole thing might open you up a little more?"

"Talking with Carolyn, or going out with Chase?" Jessie was losing track of the conversation. Even though she was here with Amanda, her mind was on Chase.

"The thing with Chase. Carolyn said that many dominants help their submissive's gain confidence."

"The truth is I don't really know what I'd be getting into with him. The whole sex thing is a lot on its own, but adding in those other things we saw? I'm not even sure I could do the sex." Laughing, embarrassed, she shrugged.

"Have you told him you're still a virgin?" Amanda whispered the last word.

"Not in so many words, I guess. I did explain my relationship with Greg." She just assumed he had figured that out during their conversation.

"At least he knows where you're coming from."

Their meal arrived, and they ate in companionable silence. Both of them refused dessert, but did order some red wine. "I just want you to be happy. I guess you've got to go with your own intuition here. If it doesn't work out at least you can say you went out with a hot, sexy dungeon master." Amanda chuckled.

Jessie shook her head and laughed as well. "There's always that to consider." She'd lived the last few years of her life in a bubble. Maybe it was time she stepped out and explored a little. But was stepping out in this capacity the right way to go?

"And of course you'll have some incredible stories to share with the ladies. You can't forget that one, either."

"Who knows? Maybe someday I'll even write a book about my experiences." Jessie giggled. The thought of writing a romance novel with her as the heroine was crazy.

"You never know. I've got to get back to work. Daddy is having a board meeting this afternoon and demands my presence." Rolling her eyes, she stood up.

"Well, tell your dad I said hello, and I look forward to seeing him at the staff meeting next week." Standing, she grabbed her purse and left the tip before Amanda could. Crawford, Amanda's father, was a brilliant man, and she didn't understand why her friend didn't worship him as she did.

"I'll tell him you'll take over running the company when he retires, and then he'll still let me have my inheritance." Shaking her head, she smirked.

They parted ways and Jessie drove back to her apartment, thinking about the decision she needed to make. She decided to do what she normally did when she needed to make a choice. Sitting at the kitchen table, she made a pros and cons list. On the pro list she had quite a few items, not the least being she got to date an extraordinarily handsome man. The only real con was the fact that she didn't really understand what happened in a relationship like this.

Sitting back in the chair, tapping her pen against her chin, she concluded she'd have to talk with him about what he wanted from her. With that decision made, she picked up the phone and called. She got his answering service, and left a quick message before walking back to her bedroom to work.

Several hours later, her project was back on schedule, even if her eyes were starting to water from staring at the computer screen. She really did love her job, and being able to focus again was a huge relief. Since making the decision to at least hear Chase out, her thoughts were much more settled.

CHAPTER FIVE

Family Affairs

Meeting with his father today had him on edge. The last conversation they'd had, he'd sensed there was something he was holding back. The two of them were complete opposites. George was very conservative, and Chase considered himself a liberal. Even with their differences, Chase couldn't fault the home he'd been raised in. His father had done very well raising a young boy on his own after his mother lost her life in childbirth. Mutual respect, a lesson his father had ingrained in him from an early age.

It took some time for his father to accept his lifestyle. They never discussed what went on inside his club, but George helped him develop his first business plan. Pulling up to the five-star restaurant, he handed his keys over to the valet and with a sinking feeling in his gut, he took a deep breath.

Walking inside, he was met by the host and gave his name for the reservation he was sure his father had made. Told his father was already waiting inside, he followed a waiter to his table. Forcing away the ominous feeling, he sat down, and then smiled warmly. "Nice to see you, sir." Taking his napkin off the table, he placed it in his lap.

"Good to see you, you're looking well, Chase."

"As are you, dad." Chase ordered a sweet tea, knowing his father didn't approve of alcohol. He tried to appease him in that department. "How have you been?" George looked like he'd aged years in the last few months.

"That's why I wanted to meet with you today." Sitting back in his chair, he frowned. "My physician diagnosed me with malignant Mesothelioma, and unfortunately, the prognosis doesn't look great."

Leave it to his dad to just lay the truth on the table, he thought. Chase felt like the world had just slipped out of the realm of reality. It took him several minutes to control his emotions enough to speak. He wasn't a weak man, but the thought of losing his father almost made him faint. "How bad is it, dad?" This was the man who had raised him and taught him how to be a decent person.

"I didn't want to say anything until I knew for sure, but it's end stage so I'm refusing chemotherapy." Shrugging he continued, "Maybe three months."

"What if you decide to do the therapy?" Chase knew his father well enough to know he wouldn't even consider that. He'd been a healthy man most of his life, with a contempt for hospitals. George was also prideful, this would seem like a weakness to him.

"You are well aware how I feel about poisoning my body like that, son. If the good lord is ready for me, then I'll just live out what time he's left for me without all those drugs." Smiling bravely, he took a sip of his water.

Chase wanted to order him not to be so stubborn, but an argument with him wasn't going to happen, or change his stance. "You know I'm here for you," he said. "Just let me know what I can do to help you through this." He had to choke out the words. The thought of losing him was devastating, but he had an immense respect for his father, and knew he expected him to be strong.

"Well there is something. I know you're fond of that club you own," he glanced down at his glass, "but I don't want my company being handed over to some stranger when I make my way home to be with your mother. It would give me a great sense of peace if you'd take over when my time comes."

He knew what it cost his father to ask. How could he refuse? The club was important to him, but he was growing tired of the scene. "If that's really what you want, you know I won't refuse." He knew his father's company better than anyone, having worked for him years after college and until the time he'd bought Sensation's. It wasn't that he didn't like the company. He'd just wanted to do something that was his dream and not his old man's. But his needs were inconsequential at the moment.

"Thank you, son. I appreciate you agreeing to keep my legacy going." Smiling, he raised his cup.

Did he really think he'd refuse him? "No, dad, thank you for showing me what honor and respect means." He forced a smile, raising his own cup. He was numb as he thought about losing this man who had taught him so much. He wouldn't show his emotions. In what little time they had left together, he planned on making sure his father knew just how much his son loved him.

"I didn't do anything any self-respecting father wouldn't have done for their son. I'm not sure how long I'll be able to keep working, so if you're sure about this, I would like to get the ball rolling as soon as possible."

His head started to pound. He needed to find someone to take over the club quickly, but he had a candidate in mind. His main concern now was helping ease his father's worries. "I want you to be able to relax and take things easy right now," he said, "so you just let me know what needs to be done, and I'll see to it that it happens." George nodded and his mouth rose in an attempted smile. Chase knew that was for his benefit.

"We need to set up a meeting with the lawyers and get all the details tied down, and son, I want you to know how much I appreciate this."

They enjoyed the rest of their lunch and restricted themselves to topics that had nothing to do with George's illness. Hoping to take his mind off the terrible situation, Chase turned the topic to football. It was one topic they could both agree on. They both were fans of the same college program.

Chase left the lunch feeling the weight of the world on his shoulders. He managed to keep his emotions in check until he made it back to his home, and then for the first time since he'd become a man, he sat down in his study and cried. The knowledge that his father was leaving this world, sat heavy on his heart.

He remembered fondly the first time his father had taken him to the plant, and the pride that shone in his eyes. As a single father, George had brought him there on school vacations and during the summer. Everything he knew about business was because of that great man.

Turning the club over wasn't as disheartening as he'd thought. He loved the lifestyle, but he no longer craved a public dungeon. Maybe he was just getting older, but the thought of settling down with one woman to enjoy this, appealed to him. Thoughts of one particularly enchanting woman suddenly filled his mind.

His thoughts strayed to Jessie a lot these days. There was something special about her, and he wanted to discover her secrets. Knowing the news his father gave him wasn't conducive to rational thinking, he brushed aside all thoughts about her. He had much more important things to worry about at the moment. With that thought, he kicked off his shoes and climbed into bed. The stress of the day had made his head pound, and rest proved impossible.

CHAPTER SIX

Jessie waited for the phone call that never came, and wondered if Chase had decided to just not bother with her. It hurt a little more than she would have thought to know he wasn't really interested in her. After taking a run, grabbing a shower, and checking again for messages, she sat down with her new best friend of the moment, rocky road ice cream.

Finishing half the cartoon, she felt on the verge of vomiting, and it did little to help with her depression. "Some friend you are," she spoke to the box as if it were responsible for her bad mood, before placing it back in the freezer.

Sebastian rubbed against her ankle, his silver and white fur, soft against the bare flesh. Picking him up in her arms, she nuzzled her face against his back. "I guess that's what I get for thinking about a man." Sebastian's answering purr seemed to say he agreed with her.

Two sappy romances later, she turned off the television. Watching movies was something she didn't do often, and it was just more proof of her depressing mood. Finally she made a decision.

Sitting around moping about him, definitely wasn't going to help, so she called Amanda. They agreed to meet at her house later for drinks, and she forced herself to keep up a cheerful disposition that she really wasn't feeling. As the evening arrived, she couldn't help but wonder how she'd so misread the signs Chase was giving off last night. It never entered her mind that something might have come up.

She dressed casually for her visit to Amanda's and on the drive over she hoped her company would help cheer her up a bit. Several glasses of wine later, they sat on her oversized couch, and her friend seemed just as puzzled as she was about him never returning the call.

"It just doesn't make sense; the man was practically eating you up with his eyes at the book club." Curling her legs under her on the couch, Amanda scrunched up her face.

"I guess maybe he realized I wasn't worth his time." She gave a small laugh to show that she was joking, but internally that was how she felt.

"That's not funny Jessie, you know what? I'm going to call Carolyn and let her know how poor her judgment in men is!" Sliding down to the arm of the couch she picked up the phone and dialed her number.

"That's not very nice Amanda," but gave up trying to convince her to not call since she was apparently ignoring her at the moment. Sipping on her wine, she decided that it was time she started making herself available again. It was apparent her heart had healed enough to want to date again, and even though the thought of meeting strange men wasn't comfortable, she knew she didn't want to be alone forever.

Amanda tapped her manicured nail against the phone receiver, waiting for Carolyn to pick up. "I want you to know that your friend is not everything you say he is."

"Which friend are we talking about?" Carolyn slid on her heels, and checked her reflection in the mirror before walking across her bedroom.

"Chase, who else, Jessie is just heartbroken that he didn't call her back."

"You've lost me Amanda, what has Chase done and why should Jessie care?" Sighing into the phone Carolyn waited.

"He asked her out last night and then didn't call her back today; you know how hard Jessie takes things."

"Hello, sitting right here, he just isn't interested, it's not the end of the world." Amanda was her best friend, but even she could admit that she enjoyed stretching the truth when it suited her.

"I'd love to talk about this Amanda, but I'm heading to Chase's now, there's been a family emergency. I'll have to explain the details after I talk with him about it."

"Oh," Amanda's attitude changed immediately. "Well I hope everything's okay."

"I'll let you know later, and tell Jessie I'm sure with everything going on he just didn't think to call her. I really need to run, we'll talk soon." Carolyn hung up the phone.

"Apparently something's going on with Chase's family and Carolyn is headed over to discuss it with him. She said to let you know that it wasn't you, he just had a lot on his mind."

She was more than a little relieved knowing he hadn't just blown her off, but now she was worried about him. They didn't know each other well enough for her to call Carolyn back and ask for answers, but she hoped everything was alright. She didn't know him well enough, that really struck home.

With the missing phone call issue solved, she and Amanda finished off a bottle of wine and Amanda in-

sisted she stay over since she was obviously too inebri-
ated to drive. Jessie wasn't about to argue with her
since two cups of wine were usually her limit.

The wine made her feel a little more open. "So what
do you think about Chase?" She considered Amanda an
expert on the subject of men, so she trusted her opin-
ions.

Drinking another sip of wine, she tapped her finger
to her chin. "I can't put my finger on that one honestly. Knowing about his desires, I would like to label him
as a womanizer, but after seeing how respectful he acted, both at the dungeon and the book club meeting, it
doesn't fit."

"He's treated me with nothing but respect, of course
we've only met two times." Her head feeling light from
the alcohol wasn't really allowing her to use her reasoning skills at the moment.

"There's no doubt he's hot as hell to look at," laughing at Jessie she waggled her eyebrows. "I think he's
complicated. That definition seems to fit, yes complicated."

"In other words you don't know what to think about
him, other than the fact he comes in a pretty package,"
giggling at the thought of her best friend being confounded over a man made her heart feel a little lighter.

"I'm sure it's just the wine," she smirked taking another long drink. "Bad boy with a heart, that's how I'll label him."

Amanda always enjoyed categorizing men. It was something of a hobby for her but bad boy just really didn't fit Chase. "I don't know, I mean I basically offered myself up to him and he encouraged me to go home and think about it, bad boy?"

"Well considering the things he does for pleasure, I wouldn't call him an altar boy," snorting wine out her nose, as she laughed so loud she could barely breathe.

Jessie couldn't argue with that, and the sight of her friend with wine all over her face had her giggling hysterically. That and the overindulgence in wine was almost too much.

Amanda stood and walked to the bar, still laughing as she pulled out a napkin, wiping her face. "So seriously, were you really going to allow him to do some of those things to you?" Her expression grew serious as the words were spoken.

The look on her face was enough to stop her own laughter. "The thought of him touching me was enough to make me not care what he did." Gazing back into her best friend's face she wondered about her own sanity for a moment.

"He turns you on that much?" Amanda's eyes widened.

Shaking her head at the surprise in her eyes, she nodded. "I know it's crazy but when he's near me, I want to fall into his arms and just give in to every ounce of pleasure he can make me feel."

"Damn you've got it bad." Grinning again, she sat down on the couch. "Have you ever thought you just might need to get laid?"

Slapping her friend on the arm, she laughed again. "You know my feelings on that, I want more than just casual sex."

"Yeah but tied up having your ass spanked to get it?" Cringing, she wrinkled her nose.

"I think it's not having to tell him what I really want. Does that make sense?" She wasn't sure she understood why she was suddenly willing to experiment with this.

Amanda nodded. "I guess there's that. I could see you not being able to put into words what satisfies you. From what you've told me about your relationship with Greg, you never experimented outside of a little petting."

"Exactly, so the thought of him taking control in that aspect isn't all that frightening to me. Now the other stuff like we saw in the dungeon, that makes me want to tuck my tail between my legs and never find out if the other stuff is worth it."

"I don't know, I think I might enjoy a little experimentation in that area. Speaking of, I got an offer from one of the men at Chase's club." Waggling her eyebrows, her mouth lifted in a smile.

"And you were going to tell me when?" Amanda never held out on telling her about her dates before.

"We only went out to dinner, but he was a first-timer at Sensation's the night we were there. He seems like a decent enough guy, so we'll see."

"Tell me more," Amanda's face was harboring a secretive little grin and she was intrigued.

"He's a lawyer at one of the firms' downtown, and says that he's been curious about this for a while. Honestly he just seems like an average guy, of course he's drop dead gorgeous." She shrugged.

"So when are you meeting him again?" Maybe this was the one for Amanda, she really hoped for once this was a nice guy. She always dated the nice looking ones, but so far they'd all failed to strike a spark in her heart.

"He's cooking for me at my place this weekend. A man that can cook, now that's a first for me. We know the same people, his company has even done business with daddy. It's odd we haven't met before now."

"Well be careful, I mean just because the guys a lawyer doesn't mean he isn't a closet jerk." It was funny to be giving advice to Amanda when she really didn't have any past experience with dating outside of Greg.

"I will but he's a professional, I'm sure he's just as worried about his career as I am about daddy discovering I went to Sensations." Laughing, she rolled her eyes.

Yawning, she realized the wine was really catching up with her. "Still, be careful all the same." Standing up she stretched. "I think I'm going to call it night."

"Same here, I've got the guest room all made up." Waving, Amanda walked off to her bedroom.

Knowing her way around her friend's house by memory, she found the other room and quickly undressed. As her head found the pillow, she fell asleep, dreaming of Chase making love to her underneath a waterfall.

CHAPTER SEVEN

Details

Chase had explained the situation to Carolyn when she'd arrived last night. After hours of discussion, he was pleased that she would be running his company for him. There was no one better suited for the task, so at least that was one worry he could take off his mind. He was meeting with the lawyers today to sign papers on his father's company, and have other's drawn up for Carolyn for his. Stress was a mild word for what he was dealing with at the moment.

The message from Jessie wasn't found until after Carolyn had left, and he thought it would be rude to call her back so late, so he decided to try her after all the meetings today. He wasn't really in the frame of mind to start a relationship with all the changes going on in his life, but the thought of not seeing her didn't sit well with him either.

Signing the papers with the lawyer made everything seem so final, and his emotions were strung tight. There were so many things to take care of, many of which he still didn't understand especially when it came to taking care of his father's needs. He knew his father needed fulltime care, and if he was going to run the company, unfortunately it couldn't be him. He thought of hiring a private nurse, but knowing his dad, that idea was going to get shot down pretty quickly.

In the course of a day his entire life had been turned upside down, and he needed to find a way to keep his thoughts organized. Driving back to his father's business, he decided to at least call Jessie and let her know what was going on. He owed her that much, he thought. Using his overhead phone system in the car he spoke her number out loud for his car's hands free device, and waited for her to answer. When she picked up, the sound of her voice was enough to make his day a little less despairing. "Hey Jessie, I'm really sorry about not calling back last night, I had some family issues."

"Carolyn told me something was going on, are you okay?"

He didn't want to burden her with his problems, but it was nice to at least hear her voice. "I'm fine. My dad is having some medical issues." That was giving enough information without burdening her.

"Oh Chase, I'm so very sorry, what can I do to help?"

"Honestly there's not much anyone can do, he's refusing chemotherapy so it's just waiting on the inevitable I guess." As much as he hated to admit it, it was nice being able to share his problems with someone else.

"Cancer? Oh Chase, you must be going through hell right now."

"It's not one of the better times in my life," he spoke solemnly, the kindness in her voice made him want to continue talking about it, which shocked him somewhat.

"Do you want to have coffee and talk about it? I know when I lost my mom, if it weren't for Amanda I'm not sure I could have lived through it."

Torn between taking advantage of her generous heart, and needing to be a strong man, he couldn't deny wanting to see her. "Could we do it at my place later tonight? I'm really not interested in being around a crowd of people at the moment."

"Of course, just give me directions and a time."

He gave her directions, "Would eight be alright? I've still got to sort some things out at my father's office, and I'm not sure how long that's going to take."

"Eight sounds fine, and if you need to make it later, give me a call."

"Thanks Jessie, I really appreciate this, to be honest I don't want to be alone right now." How weak and pathetic did that sound, he shook his head. He was supposed to be a dominant male and here he was acting like some little boy who needed to be broken from the teat."

"I'll see you then, and if you need me to pick up anything on the way in, let me know."

"Your beautiful face is all I need," he tried to force himself out the funk he was in at least long enough to hopefully make her smile. "I'll see you tonight." Ending the call he breathed a sigh of relief.

Driving back to his father's offices he smiled for the first time today. It was amazing how just speaking to her made the dark cloud that seemed to be surrounding him at the moment, dissipate. Dealing with all the paperwork that afternoon wasn't as disheartening as he thought about seeing her tonight.

Several of his father's employees stopped in the office as he was organizing to give their condolences. He appreciated their gestures, but it almost made him feel like his father was already gone. At least all the records were organized to perfection. He smiled weakly remembering how meticulous his father had been about his business affairs.

He needed to set up consultations with the heads of the departments, but just didn't have it in him to arrange that yet. The next few months would require all the staff to grow accustomed to his different attitude in management, but in truth he wasn't sure they'd see that many changes. Most of what he knew about business was because of his father.

By the end of the day his head was pounding, and all he could think about was taking his mind off things for a while. He'd already called his father, and for the moment he was dealing as well as could be expected considering the circumstances. He even got him to agree to a fulltime nurse. That shocked him beyond belief. His thoughts turned back to the petite beauty joining him later tonight.

Closing his eyes, rubbing his temples to ease the ache, he imagined her blue-green eyes filled with longing looking his way. His mind conjured up a fantasy of her wearing nothing but a smile. Her small hands reached out to him, begging to be filled. His cock instantly hardened, and his hand moved to it without thought. The thought of her hand stroking him was so intense his eyes opened immediately. "Shit," he cursed, getting off at work was not an impression he wanted to give.

Standing up, he quickly gathered his briefcase and walked out of the building. Shielding his erection with the case, he shook his head. The woman was coming to his house as a friend. That was all. His mind made up, he found his car and drove home.

CHAPTER EIGHT

Feelings

Finishing up the work the office had sent over, she spent the rest of the afternoon looking up information on Mesothelioma. When she arrived at Chase's house tonight, she wanted to understand a little more about what his father was dealing with. She wasn't knowledgeable when it came to healthcare, so everything she read just seemed horrific. After her research she wondered if she were in Chase's father's position, if she wouldn't have refused the option of therapy as well.

Dressing in a pair of jeans and t-shirt, she considered comfort first. Tonight wasn't a date, she reminded herself, but an opportunity to offer some moral support to someone in need. He hadn't called back to delay the time, so she followed the directions to his home, and when she arrived she was floored at the beauty that met her eyes.

She hadn't thought about his financial status, so discovering that he lived in such opulence was a little overwhelming. She was definitely feeling underdressed as she guided the car into the circular driveway. Parking in front of the three story brownstone, she reminded herself that she wasn't here in a romantic capacity so it didn't truly matter.

Walking up to the door she was greeted by another woman. Smiling into the elderly face, she tried not to appear as nervous as she suddenly felt. "Um, I'm Jessie. I'm here to meet with Chase?"

"Chase is expecting you dear, please follow me." Smiling warmly, Louise guided her to the study.

A last minute business call had him running late and he smiled and held up a finger as he concluded his conversation. Hanging up the phone he shrugged apologetically. "Sorry I wasn't there to greet you in person Jessie," walking over he took her hands in his.

"Louise did Jessie introduce herself yet?" His housekeeper was almost like a mother to him and he treated her as part of his family. She'd been with him since he was six and had made the move with him from his father's house when he moved out on his own

"She did, and I must say she's a lovely girl."

Getting the Louise seal of approval was almost a miracle, and he chuckled feeling a little less morbid than he had for most of the day. Louise had no problem telling him if she didn't approve of someone he invited over, although she did wait until the person had left, to which he was always grateful. Louise had come to his family from Ireland and she carried that fiery disposition that he simply loved. No nonsense and honest to a fault.

It was apparent that these two people had more than just a working relationship, and Jessie was glad he at least had someone taking care of him that cared. "It's really nice to meet you Ms. Louise," she'd been raised herself to always give proper respect to the elderly.

"Just Louise, young lady, but it's nice to see that some young people still have manners. I'll bring some refreshments in." Not giving them time to respond, she left the room.

"She seems really nice," Jessie smiled and looked down at their hands, which he was still holding.

"She's a good woman, but don't let her fool you, she's got an Irish temper if you ever get on her bad side." He chuckled as he remembered some of the scolding's she'd given him as a child.

His hands felt so good in hers, and she stood awkwardly for a moment when she couldn't think of a thing to say.

Realizing that he still had her hands, he gave a rueful grin. "So would you like to sit down?" He was acting like an adolescent, as he rubbed his thumbs over the softness of her hands. Without warning the thought of how much he'd love to have those hands tied over her head as he made love to her passionately, filled his mind. He released her hands quickly, not accustomed to letting his other head lead him.

She nodded, and lowered her eyes at the intensity of his gaze. Feeling her heart race, something she was beginning to think was normal when he was around, she forced a small smile. They sat down together and there were a few minutes of awkward silence.

Jessie couldn't stop thinking of how good it felt to have his hands hold hers earlier, and he wanted to forget everything going on his life for a moment and enjoy something as normal as desiring a beautiful woman. He finally broke the silence.

"So tell me how you met Carolyn?" Great idea, he derided himself mentally. Bring up another woman when he really wanted to know more about her.

Glad to have something to talk about, instead of wondering what it would feel like if his lips found hers, she smiled. "My best friend Amanda introduced her to me when she invited me to join the book club."

"The ladies there seem very inquisitive about alternative lifestyles?" He needed to keep her talking, instead of allowing his eyes to roam over her incredible body. Hell, just being in the room with her made him ache to touch her.

Feeling a little more comfortable, she nodded. "They definitely enjoy researching what they read." That was an understatement after their trip to the dungeon.

"What about you, do you take the same interest they do with all the stories?" He smiled, and shifted on the couch, not sure this topic of conversation was conducive to keeping his testosterone in check. For reasons he couldn't explain he felt like a randy teenager at the moment.

Flushing, she considered his question for a moment. "Not really, I'm happy just accepting the fantasies for what they were." The whole BDSM thing hadn't really been something she'd thought about before walking into his club. She just accepted at face value that those books were accurate.

"So you never considered the fantasies might be something you'd like to try on your own?" Definitely not the right way to take the conversation, again he forced a smile as his jeans grew tighter.

Admitting that until him her fantasies hadn't been something she considered at all, didn't seem like the right thing to blurt out. She shrugged, and decided to turn the topic over to him. "What about you? I mean you told the group you got into this after a former girlfriend introduced you. The female master, was she the reason you wanted to own your own club?

"Dominatrix," he corrected her terminology and grinned. Resting back on the couch, he allowed his arm to rest behind her back on the top of the fabric. "I guess in a way she was. I was living in Chicago while studying for my degree. Sheila, that's the older woman, took me to a dungeon there."

She liked the feeling of knowing his arm was behind her. "So one visit to a dungeon and you were hooked?" He didn't seem like an impulsive man, her eyes rested on his face questioningly.

"Let's just say that dungeon really impressed me. I spent two years there as a patron. When I moved back here, there wasn't a club like it. So after working for my father for seven years, I'd really gotten tired of having groups of people over at my house, and decided to create something that could be used for the public."

The thought of him having a dungeon here was intriguing, if not a little frightening. "You didn't like sharing your private space then?" She had no idea what that was like, but couldn't say she'd feel very comfortable having a group of people bombarding her personal space.

"It wasn't so much that I didn't like it, I consider myself very sociable, but I enjoy having personal space as well. It just made more sense to give something back to the community that embraced me. With Sensation's it's easier to offer access during longer periods of times, and it grew beyond anything I'd expected." The surge of people exploring the lifestyle had grown beyond his imagination, and since it was no longer such a taboo subject, he expected even more growth in the future.

She wasn't sure why she was so fascinated with this subject, but she felt comfortable now. Pulling her feet up under her on the couch, she smiled. "You seem so relaxed when you talk about this? When you first started doing all these things, weren't you nervous?"

His response was delayed when Louise entered the room with a tray of snacks and a pitcher of sweet tea. "Thank you Louise," the woman truly was one of the few constants in his life, he thought to himself.

"You're welcome, now if you young people don't need me, I think I'll retire for the night."

Louise had definitely picked up the Southern drawl over her years here, and mixed with the Irish brogue, it was quiet charming to him. "I think we can manage Louise, enjoy your evening."

"It was very nice to meet you," Jessie gave a smile.

"Very nice to meet you, young lady," with a small wave of her hand, Louise left them to enjoy their night.

"She really seems like a good woman," Jessie commented as they were left alone once again.

"She is, Louise has been with me since I was a child, and kept me in line more than my own father at times." He chuckled. "But back to your other question, yes I was nervous in the beginning. I had no idea what I was doing, and at first I thought this was just a way to get women to do things I wanted."

He saw her eyes widen at his comment and chuckled loudly. "Believe me I've discovered a wealth of information since those days. As a young man I just didn't know enough to consider how this could be more than just sex or bossing people around."

She wanted to ask about his father, but was fascinated by the insight into the man sitting before her too. She reasoned that maybe taking his mind off the other might help him more. "So you don't boss people around anymore?" Raising an eyebrow she grinned.

"Oh believe me I can be very bossy," he grinned, "but I channel it to help the submissive, instead of just being an overbearing bully. That's how I see some of these people entering the lifestyle today and honestly it just makes me angry. There's nothing worse to me than a man who enjoys demeaning women calling himself a dominant." It was another reason he considered stepping out of the public lifestyle. Too many posers these days.

"I don't get it, isn't that the entire point of tying them up or bending them to your will?"

"Not in my world now, when I choose a submissive, it's because I know I can offer her something in return for giving me her gift, and I'm not talking materialistically. Say for instance with you, if you were my submissive I would help you gain more confidence."

She was that easy to read, she frowned at the thought. "Why do you think I lack confidence?"

"It's in the way you look at your hands or feet during a conversation, and how you slouch your shoulders." He hoped he wasn't offending her, but she did ask. "You're a beautiful woman Jessie, when you walk into any room, you should know that and be proud of who you are."

Being told she slouched didn't make her feel very good, but his compliment to her beauty was nice. "So I'm a sloucher?" Giving a little smirk, she wondered if he realized how rude it was to say that.

Throwing his head back he laughed deeply. "No I said you slouched, but that doesn't make you a sloucher to me, it just means you need to gain a little more confidence in your appearance."

"So you would teach me how to have more confidence. How would you do that?" She wasn't going to argue the fact. She knew she didn't feel good about herself.

"I'd probably make you walk around naked in my dungeon downstairs every single time we met here until you realized how beautiful you are in my eyes." He gave a wink, wondering how she was going to deal with his comment.

The thought of doing that made her heart fall into her stomach and she could only stare at him. To say the very least he was blunt. "You're joking right?" When she was finally able to find her voice, she had to know the truth.

"No Jessie, I'm not joking at all. If a woman can prance around naked in front of her lover, then she should have no problem walking around confident when she's clothed."

"What other things would you do, hypothetically speaking of course, if I were your submissive?" Did she really want to know the answer? Being naked all the time was already a deal breaker, *wasn't it*?

"I'd really have to think about it Jessie, but I'd discover all your weaknesses and help you rise above them. To me that's what being a true dominant is really about."

"So once you had accomplished everything you wanted with a submissive, then what, it's over?" She really didn't understand how any of this worked for him.

"The submissive's in my past have been ones I've trained for others, so a permanent relationship has been out of the question." Again, he thought of having someone in his life on a long term basis. "But I'd like to think that none of us ever stop learning Jessie, so you never truly finish."

"So it's not about the sex to you?" She found that a little difficult to believe, the man was obviously gorgeous, and he had to have needs.

"It's not 'just' about the sex Jessie. Don't get me wrong, the sexual aspect of this is mind blowing. For the submissive it takes away all the worries about doing the wrong thing, which I personally believe inhibits women from enjoying sexuality to its greatest potential. And sure, I enjoy being in complete control of the situation. Knowing that I decide whether or not my submissive finds sexual gratification is a huge turn on for me."

She was trying to digest all he was saying and honestly it wasn't as frightening to her as he explained it more. The thought of a male taking control in the bedroom wasn't a turn off at all. "But the whole pain aspect, I know you said it was something you worked up to, but what's the point?"

"The pain isn't truly painful. I know that's a little hard to understand for someone who hasn't experienced it. Of course again that depends on the two people in the relationship."

She really didn't have any idea what he was talking about, and she glanced at him questioningly. "Pain is not painful, that seems like a complete oxymoron?"

Chuckling at her response, he tried to explain. "You could ask any dominant what his definition of a BDSM relationship means, and it would probably be different in some way. There are those that just enjoy pain for pains sake. I just don't subscribe to that and like to deal more with the bondage and the relationship side of the equation, and focus on the pleasure aspects. Now I will say punishment does have its uses in this though, and I don't think that part of it is usually pleasurable."

"I'm confused again sorry, so the punishment is actually painful? Why would you punish someone if you truly cared about them?" She leaned over and rested her elbows on her knees then rested her face in her palms.

Sitting back more comfortably on the couch, he considered how to word this so she would understand his perspective. "People are usually motivated to do the right thing when there is a negative consequence hanging in the balance. For example most people finish their work on time, because knowing if they don't it could result in them being fired. With punishment and this type of lifestyle, say I wanted you to learn a certain type of behavior because I knew it would help you in life and you were having trouble remembering what I was asking you to do, punishment could be a quick reminder."

"I can understand completing a task on time and being reprimanded, but being scolded by your lover? That sounds a little like a parental relationship."

He laughed out loud at her description. "Trust me Jessie, if I had you draped over my knee the last thing you'd be thinking about was me in a father capacity." He could actually imagine having her that way and fought to keep that image closed off.

Thinking about it, she couldn't really picture herself seeing him in that capacity either. "So you punish your lover. Don't you worry that she'll just get mad and make you sleep on the couch?" Imagining him spanking her wasn't really as frightening as it should be. In fact it gave her heart a little flutter.

He was glad she was discussing this. He noticed how calm she was, that was more than pleasing. "That's the real difference between this and say a normal relationship Jessie, at least in my world. Where a couple in a vanilla relationship would probably go to bed angry with each other after screaming out all their frustrations or refusing to discuss them at all, with this that's just not an option."

"Being open and honest from the beginning, teaches both parties how to communicate with each other. With some of the toys or other implements we use, being anything less than completely honest can not only be painful, but also dangerous. The point is everything is done for pleasure, but while discovering what truly pleasures a submissive you are learning also about their limits."

She still wasn't sure she completely understood his reasoning, even if some of it made sense. "So what do you really get out of this Chase?" It was well and good to discuss what he liked to think he could offer a submissive, but there had to be something he took away as well.

"Outside of making sure that I help my submissive find pleasure, I teach her ways to please me. I know that may sound strange Jessie, but imagine having every need you had fulfilled, how do you think you'd respond to the man responsible for opening your eyes to that?"

She stopped to consider what he was saying. "I guess knowing how hard he worked to please me, I'd probably want to give back in the same way." It did make sense in some strange way she'd never thought to consider before.

"Exactly, that's what makes this type of relationship truly work. Yes, the submissive gives the gift of submission to the dominant, but in return she discovers passion in herself that she may have never discovered without his guidance. So being an egotistical alpha male really doesn't fit the definition of a true dominant. The dominant does control the situation, but if he's not pleasing his submissive, he won't have one for long to dominate."

It seemed so much simpler than she'd originally thought when reading this in her romance novels. Everything she had read about showed these men with troubled pasts and their need to be in control of everything to make their lives more meaningful. With Chase it just seemed like he wanted a partnership that was based on two people giving each other different gifts and complimenting each other's lives.

"Would you like to take a tour of my personal dungeon?" All this talk about his lifestyle had him thinking about sharing it with her. The blunt question was as much of shock to him as he was sure it was to her.

She was admittedly curious about his dungeon, and nodded. "As long as you promise to let me leave once you have me all alone down there. I would love to see it." Grinning at her own joke, she stood up ready for the tour.

"I don't know Jessie, locking you in my dungeon is more than a little tempting we'll have to see." Taking her hand in his, he walked her out of the living room to the basement door. "Are you sure you trust me to let you leave later?" He couldn't help joking around with her since she made the comment about being locked up first.

Smiling at him, she nodded. Oddly enough she wasn't nervous as they made their way down the long flight of stairs. It definitely wasn't the dark gloomy space she'd expected, and while some of the furniture was a little strange to her, lit with soft lights it appeared warmer, and more inviting than the room at the club.

"Most of these things you saw at Sensation's. I do like to think that my equipment here is a little less basic." He'd decorated the dungeon with the things he enjoyed playing with and left out some of the things that didn't appeal. It had a cross, spanking beach, and exam table, and then of course the suspension bars. He actually preferred the softer wool-lined cuffs if he was playing personally, but those didn't work well in the dungeon at Sensation's.

"I do believe a little payback is in order for letting you shackle me to the cross." He gave a playful smirk, and motioned to the cross. "Don't worry. I'll let you leave your clothes on, this time." Laughing at her shocked expression, he shook his head. "Nothing will happen here that you don't want Jessie."

Her heart rate increased as she walked over to the cross, but in excitement not fear. The truth was she knew he wouldn't hurt her. She was curious to know what it felt like to be as helpless as he had been the other night. Standing awkwardly on the platform of the cross she held her arms up. "Like this?"

Smiling patiently, he took one of her wrists and secured it in the fur-lined cuff, then entrapped the other. "Just like that," he spoke soothingly. Kneeling down he lifted her leg to position her ankle at the right spot and secured it, then tapped her other leg until she opened her stance wide enough so he could secure the other. Standing up, he glanced over her and smiled broadly. "The only thing that could make you more beautiful right now, would be if you wearing nothing at all."

She flushed and lowered her eyes, embarrassed, but pleased somewhat by the compliment. Holding her breath, she allowed the sensation of being completely helpless to wash over her. She wasn't afraid at all. Excited yes, but definitely not afraid.

Placing his hand under her chin, he lifted it. "Don't look down Jessie. I want to see those mesmerizing eyes." Keeping his hand under her chin, their gazes met and he was floored by the response of his body. Almost instantaneously, he was aroused, something he hadn't felt so quickly since he was much younger. "What you make me feel Jessie." Chase smiled ruefully and lowered his lips to hers tenderly.

The touch of his warm lips against hers made her sigh. The feel of his tongue sliding into her mouth and touching hers was enough to make her body ache for more. It had been so long since anyone had kissed her.

She leaned into him, as much as she could with the restrains, demanding more.

Moving his large hands to each side of her face, he held it as he deepened the kiss. The taste of her was exquisite, and he couldn't get enough. After several long minutes of enjoying her, he pulled back. "Tell me to stop Jessie. If you don't I'm going to want so much more from you than a simple kiss." He kept his hands on her face staring deeply into her eyes.

"I don't want you to stop," she whispered softly, unable to look away even if she wanted to.

That was all the response he needed, and he kissed her again. His hands moved from her face to trace up her arms until their hands were entwined. Pressing his body against hers, he wanted her to know how aroused he was by their simple act, so she would understand just how much he craved her.

The feel of his hard body against hers was incredible and she whimpered at the sensations moving through her body at the contact. It wasn't enough. She needed to feel his hands on her. Biting gently down on his lips, she showed him without words just how much she wanted him.

The small action moved straight to his groin, and he knew he had to get her off this cross. With skillful precision, he lowered to her ankles, releasing them, and moved to her wrists to undo the buckles as well. "The cross just won't work for how I want to touch you right now honey." Smiling, he lifted her over his shoulder, and carried her to the exam table.

Chuckling at his cave man act, the laughter stopped when he careful placed her on the table sitting up. She could see by the intensity of his eyes that he planned on taking this as far as she would allow. Without thinking, for perhaps the first time in her life, she lifted her t-shirt over her head. Without words, she was giving him her consent. Jessie tossed the shirt carelessly aside, nibbling her lower lip, but refusing to break eye contact.

There was nothing sexier in this world, he thought of her reaction. Chase allowed his eyes to drink in the perfection of her skin for a moment. The tiny lacy bra she wore didn't hide much, but even that was more than he was willing to allow. Lowering his lips, he captured her mouth again. His fingers quickly moved to the small clasp of the flimsy garment, undoing it before pulling the straps off her shoulders and standing back to cast it away.

Her hands automatically shielded her body from his eyes. The shake of his head made her rethink the action, and she nervously lowered her hands to clench the leather table.

"More beautiful than words." Her handful sized mounds were just perfect in his mind and fit perfectly with the petite beauty she was. He reached over to cup the light weight of her breasts, and then rubbed his thumbs over the coral-colored peaks. Pinching the hardened pebbles, her soft moan of pleasure echoed in his mind, fuelling him on. Lowering his mouth, he suckled deeply, then allowed his teeth to graze over her nipple, enjoying her response. He loved how she arched into his touch.

Tossing back her long black hair, she closed her eyes at the sensation of his teeth scraping over her enflamed flesh. It sent a spark of pleasure straight from her breast down to her core. It was unlike any other feeling she'd felt before. Her breath caught in her throat as his fingers tugged lightly on her other nipple, and she cried out, overwhelmed at the intensity.

His mouth trailed down to her quivering abdomen, and he knew that the jeans had to go. Raising his head, he spoke with gravel to his voice that wasn't there before. "Lay back honey," it was a soft demand and he was pleased that she responded so quickly.

Chase unsnapped her jeans, and lowered the zipper. She swore the sound of her pounding heart echoed in the room. When he tugged down, she raised her hips instinctively allowing him easier accesses. The material rested at her knees. She felt him pulling off her tennis shoes and socks, before removing the thick fabric of her jeans. He tossed them away.

Leaving her in just the small scrap of fabric that covered her sex, his mouth lowered down to her abdomen again. His tongue traced an outline around her navel before delving in. The way she tensed was precious, he thought. She had no idea the things he would do to her body before this night ended. For now, he needed to please more than he wanted to tease. His tongue moved to trace a line right above the band of her bikini briefs.

What was he doing to her, she thought at the feel of his tongue? His hands were pushing under her hips, lifting them. She cried out loudly as he spread her legs wide. Chase placed them over his shoulders, and his mouth found her core. Only the thin fabric of her underwear was between them and she tensed in both pleasure and a small fission of fear knowing where this was headed. No one had ever kissed her this way, and it was overwhelming at how quickly her body responded.

The scrap of lace had to go he decided. Without rational thought, he pulled it apart easily with his large hands, destroying the flimsy material. Her soft gasp at his action demanded he show her how much pleasure he could give her.

Her last barrier being removed was as shocking as they way he'd destroyed it. His tongue delving into her removed any thoughts of his behavior from her mind though. She wanted this, wanted him, and gentleness just didn't enter the equation.

If he thought the taste of her mouth was incredible, the sweet essence of her core was unbelievable. She was so wet and ready, his cock throbbed with need. Her body was pure perfection. Chase knew at this rate he wasn't going to last long enough to pleasure her if he didn't find some control. Spearing his tongue into the sweetness of her flesh, and retreating again, wasn't enough, he demanded more.

Grasping his thick hair in his hands, she lifted her hips off the table to offer him her body. Soft cries of pleasure escaped her lips. She surrendered to the magic of his mouth. "Please," she cried out pulling his hair unconsciously.

Her small hands tugging at his hair forced a primitive growl from his throat. Even that small touch was more than he could deal with if he was not going to fulfill just his needs tonight. That wasn't an option. Lifting his head, he whispered strongly. "Don't move!"

She watched as he walked over to a small chest. Her legs were still splayed open on the table, and she closed them quickly. *What was he doing*? She was worried, some of the early passion receded at the thought of what he might be pulling out of that chest. He came back with a scarf and a tiny little silver object that she could only describe as a bullet.

"I want to tie your hands Jessie," he spoke soothingly, "I can't think with you touching me, and I want to bring you pleasure tonight." The way she nibbled her lower lip, made him consider rethinking the idea, he didn't want to frighten her. Her small nod made him feel somewhat relieved, and he carefully bound her hands together with the silken scarf. "Promise me you'll keep your hands above your head."

Again she nodded, wide-eyed, raising her bound wrists over her head and watching his moves intently. Her breath was so shallow at the moment, it was almost painful. His reassuring kiss did a little to help her relax, and she forced herself to take a few deep breaths.

So damn precious, he thought, seeing how nervous she was. He wanted her to be on the same page again, and moved his mouth back to her breast to suckle deeply. As she closed her eyes and arched her back, he was relieved that his stopping mid-game, so to speak, hadn't killed her desire. Sliding back down her body, he pulled her firm thighs over his shoulder again and lightly teased her core with his tongue. He hoped the small vibrator would bring her closer to his own state of arousal. Lifting his head, Chase switched it on, lightly touching it to her clit.

At the feel of the strong buzz against her flesh, she nearly lifted off the table. She'd never used toys before and the sensation was overwhelming. She didn't know whether to scoot away or press closer as the incredible feeling vibrated through her sex. Crying out softly, her body didn't need to think as it responded instantly.

The throbbing ache continued to increase until it felt like a pressure was building that demanded release. "Chase please," she cried out desperately.

The sound of his name was more of a turn on than he would have imagined. He continued to tease her with the vibrator and allowed a long finger to slide into her silken flesh, delving deeply. She was so tight that he groaned as her flesh gripped him.

Slowly moving his finger in and out, he focused all his attention on her sex. He needed her to find release as much as he wanted to give it to her. When she finally peaked, and the soft cry of pleasure left her lips, he knew he had to be inside of her. Pulling his finger from her clenching flesh, he tossed the vibrator away carelessly. "Jessie, tell me you're protected honey." As much as he wanted her, he didn't want to risk an unplanned pregnancy here.

Trying to come down from the high long enough to think, she shook her head no. Jessie hadn't even thought about protection. She hadn't thought either that the chance of them making love tonight was an option.

He stood up quickly and kicked off his shoes. Reaching into his pants, pulling out his wallet, he opened it and gave a sigh of relief, "Thank God." Removing the condom packet, he slid off his jeans and underwear.

She could only watch him as he undressed. *They were really going to make love,* she thought. She'd waited for this moment as long as she could remember. Now the moment was here, she was a little nervous. She wasn't naive so she understood there would be some pain involved. Her eyes roamed over his wide, smooth chest, muscled arms and then lowered. Acknowledging the perfection of the man before her, she realized just how 'well endowed' he was. When Chase walked back to her, she tensed.

Knowing that his size was a little intimidating, he smiled. "I won't hurt you Jessie," giving a small wink he crawled up on the table between her thighs. The fact that she was trembling now, proved that she wasn't quite sure of that fact. He knew he'd have to prove it to her. Allowing his fingers to find her, he hoped he could live up to his promise. She was definitely smaller than women he'd been with in the past. Stretching her with his fingers had her mind back where it belonged and on the pleasure he was giving.

It was so hard to think when he was stroking her body just the right way, making her ache again for the release he'd given earlier. Arching her hips up she met each delicious slide of his long digits. It wasn't enough. Jessie felt stretched and ached, she wanted even more. Whimpering in need, she wished he would stop this torment and make her his.

The soft sounds escaping her lips were all the encouragement he needed. Removing his fingers from her clenching flesh, Chase moved over her small frame. "I want to see your eyes when I take you Jessie." He hoped the words weren't as harsh as they felt, since he was on the edge of his control. Those beautiful, blue-green eyes met his, and he guided his cock into her silken paradise. He drove forward with one long thrust. The soft cry of pain that left her lips, and the small resistance he felt in her trembling flesh, left no question in his mind about what gift she'd just given him. He remained completely still, deeply embedded as he fought to control his own needs.

Even expecting the burning pain that came with making love the first time, didn't stop the cry that escaped, or the way she tensed against the invasion. It was so much different than what she had expected, and she wasn't sure at the moment if that was a good or bad thing. Biting her lip hard, she was glad he wasn't moving as her body attempted to adjust to the strange fullness.

"I guess I broke my promise." He smiled down into her tear-filled eyes, wishing he could take that pain away. "Forgive me?" He hadn't known she was a virgin, and he'd have to think about that later, right now she was his only concern.

She nodded and attempted to smile back. The burning sensation lessened, and she moved her hips slightly to see what it would feel like. The groan that escaped him, and noticing the light sheen of sweat that covered his brow, made her realize how hard it was for him to stay still. It wasn't horrible, she decided, in fact in some odd way it felt almost good. "I think I'll forgive you if you move a little," she wanted him to at least enjoy this, even if the pleasure was over for her.

"Sweet girl," he whispered knowing damn well she was trying to appease him and actually loving her for it. "Wrap your legs around my waist honey." *He would please her if it killed him*, he thought. She complied and he slowly began moving inside her. Keeping his rhythm slow and measured was taking every ounce of self-control he possessed. His body wanted to thrust into her gripping core until simple exhaustion demanded he stop.

The feel of him stretching and filling her completely was unlike any other sensation in the world. The soreness began to recede and she felt her body build toward that pleasurable pinnacle again. Arching into his movements made the intensity even more incredible, and she knew there was even more. "Chase love me," she demanded softly. Jessie knew he was holding back for her, and she was ready to experience everything.

The tensing and releasing of her silky core gave him more indication than her words that she was finally free from pain, and he increased his pace. His body took over from his mind as he continued to thrust inside her sheath. *She was incredible*, that was the last logical thought his mind had as she found her release and clenched him so tightly within that he found his own immediately.

For long minutes she remained unmoving as he rested his weight against her. *Amazing*, a small laugh escaped as she tried to come up with a word that actually described the pleasure he'd given her. Lazily her bound hands move around his head and she ran her fingers through his thick locks.

Realizing he was probably crushing her, he slowly lifted his weight, not pleased at the small wince that came as he slid from her flesh. "Sweet Jessie, that soft laugh might just damage my ego," he winked and smiled. Carefully he untied her hands, then moved to retrieve his clothes. He wanted this petite little beauty in his bed and off this bench.

Feeling the cool air on her heated flesh she trembled. Sliding off the bench she found her clothes. "I'm sure your ego would be doing somersaults if it knew how much I enjoyed tonight." Looking away from him after her brazen comment, she quickly slid on her jeans, sans underwear.

After pulling on his pants, he quickly moved over to wrap her in an embrace. "You'll have to stroke my ego later then sweet girl, because this night hasn't even begun yet. I would however like to get you into my bed."

Chuckling at her shocked expression, he wondered if she really thought he was going to let her leave now. "Trust me. I plan on keeping you entertained until at least sunrise."

He wanted her to stay, and that just blew her away. Greg had always sent her back to her dorm room after his attempts to please her. She just assumed that's what normal couples did unless they lived together. "Sunrise?" *Would she be able to walk by then?* Her legs already felt like they would give way at any minute.

Retrieving her t-shirt off the ground, he helped her slide it over her head. "If I didn't have to show up at the office tomorrow I'd keep you here for the day." The thought of never letting her leave filled his mind, and that shocked him completely.

Not wanting to focus on those thoughts at the moment, he lifted her into his arms and carried her out of the dungeon. He didn't stop until they were in his bedroom. He sat her down on the bed carefully. "I'll run you a bath, just relax for a few minutes."

This man couldn't be real, she thought to herself. Not only had he been a generous lover, but the way he was taking care of her now seemed like something out of one of the romance books she'd read. It definitely didn't fit the description of any master she'd read about in those novels. She wanted to write those authors a letter and let them know that they were way off.

He adjusted the temperature for her bath, and moved back to be with her again. Holding out his hand, he smiled as she took it and he led her to the bathroom. When she began to undress he captured both of her hands, stopping her. "Let me do that for you." Slowly he removed her clothes again, and helped her step inside the soothing water.

Never had she felt more cherished as he washed her hair, and bathed her with the patience of a man that seemed to be enjoying the task. "Am I going to wake up and find this was all a dream?" She wasn't sure if she was asking him or herself.

"I hope not Jessie. I'm enjoying treating you the way a woman should be treated." Helping her stand, he washed her lower body, and then her sex. The tensing as he touched her core reminded him that she was newly initiated and he would have to take things slowly for the rest of the night. She sat back down and he used the sponge to drip water over her incredible body.

She'd never been this pampered. He even released the plug from the drain before holding out a towel for her to step into. His tenderness didn't stop there either. He combed out her hair and dried her body before leading her back to his oversized bed. "Do you do this with all your women?" If he did, she couldn't understand why he wasn't with someone.

Talking about other women in front of her was something he would never do. "You honored me tonight with a special gift Jessie. I just wanted to show you how much I appreciated your trust." Lowering his lips to her forehead, he kissed her chastely before walking back to the bathroom to clean up.

He didn't actually answer her question, she noted, and the self-doubt filled her mind again. What if he did do this with other women, and tonight really didn't mean anything to him? Would she be able to deal with that when the light of day came? Nibbling on her lower lip, a nervous habit she had, she pulled the towel tighter around her.

He could see instantly that she was pulling into her internal thoughts as he made it back into the room. The effect was not positive for her and he wanted to take away the insecurity that filled her eyes.

Lifting her chin with his hand, he stared down into her beautiful face. "Jessie, I have never enjoyed making love to another woman more than I have tonight." He was amazed at the depth of emotion he felt for her at that moment. A strange protectiveness overcame him. One he normally didn't feel after a night of lovemaking, no matter how in-depth it had been. It scared the hell out of him how much he wanted to claim ownership at that moment. Rationalizing internally that it could be that she was the first virgin he'd ever lain with, didn't help the feeling of possessiveness.

Her uncertainty vanished instantly at the look of honesty in his eyes, and she smiled. "I enjoyed making love with you too," she whispered somewhat embarrassed. Regardless of where this ended up she knew that the memory of him being her first would remain the rest of her life.

"I don't know Jessie. We might have to try again. You could just think you enjoyed it." He needed to get this back on a more casual level before his own thoughts made him do something they both would regret, like showing just how much of an alpha male he could be.

Her eyes widened at his words, and she was on board with that idea completely. "I guess we probably should make sure it wasn't a fluke." Where she pulled out the teasing comment, she had no idea.

"A fluke huh, we definitely can't have you wondering about that now, can we?" A mischievous glimmer entered his gaze as he thought about all the ways he could bring her pleasure without making it impossible for her to walk tomorrow. An idea came to him and he smirked. "Relax in that bed for a few minutes. I need to grab a few things and well, it might be the last time I allow you to take a break tonight." With a wink, he left her gazing at his retreating backside.

She had no idea where he was going and for a brief second she panicked. Then she recalled how tender he'd been with her tonight and relaxed again. She doubted the man who initiated her into making love so sweetly could seriously do anything she'd disagree with. Sliding into the bed she rested on the pillow and closed her eyes. Within moments she was asleep.

That was how he found her when he returned. Sleeping peacefully, he almost considered letting her rest. His mind was not agreeing with that idea, any more than his body. When he'd walked down into his dungeon, he hadn't been sure what his game plan was. When he made the decision, he knew there was no way she was going to sleep away all the erotic pleasure he had in store for her.

Quietly, he arranged all the items he'd brought upstairs on the bedside table. Turning back to her, Chase carefully bound her wrists and legs to the head and footboard of his bed. He'd installed the chain links and cuffs into his bed years ago, but had yet to put them to use. She was the first woman he'd actually brought into his bedroom. He preferred playing with submissive's only in his dungeon.

She hadn't actually agreed to be his submissive, so he hoped that she wouldn't be upset that he'd bound her in such a way. He planned on bringing her so much pleasure that the cuffs were the last thing on her mind.

With that thought playing through his head, he opened the box containing a snake bite kit and applied the rubber venom release tubes to the coral peaks of her breasts.

She moaned softly in her sleep. He smiled, thinking he would wake her up in a pleasurable way. Giving the small suction cups a moment to set, he lifted a small vial of breath drops and placed a small amount on the silken folds of her sex. Knowing how quickly the sensation would take place, he waited for her eyes to open. Hearing her soft gasp, he lowered between her legs and suckled.

She awoke to a sensation that had her gasping at the strange heat between her thighs, and then felt the soothing relief of his tongue against her flesh. It took her several moments to realize she was bound. The pleasure he was giving with his mouth took over any other thoughts. She didn't have time to consider whether or not she felt comfortable being this restricted as his tongue continued to tease. His hand lifted to her breast removing some strange rubber device. It felt so incredibly wonderful she cried out. "Chase, oh God!"

He smiled against her enflamed flesh and plunged deeply with his tongue, enjoying how responsive she was. Her hips were arching off the bed, pushing against his mouth, and he continued to lick, suckle and dart until he felt her tense. Removing the other suction device from her nipple, she came undone immediately with a loud cry of pleasure. "Falling asleep on me can be dangerous Jessie," he chuckled as he rose back up the bed beside her and placed a small kiss on her lips.

If that was his idea of dangerous she would gladly fall asleep again on him. Slowly her breathing came back to normal and she tried to think about how she felt being so exposed like this. Oddly enough it wasn't overwhelming. She instinctively knew if she asked him to remove the cuffs he would. Outside of being a little embarrassed at him seeing her body splayed out so seductively, she was fine.

He was watching her face carefully as he allowed a hand to lightly trace her abdomen. "Are you up for more Jessie girl," grinning widely as her eyes widened, he waited for her answer.

Was she ready for more? The man had already given her two of the best orgasms of her life. "Maybe?" She had no idea of what her body was capable of, but if he continued to make her feel so good, she was willing to find out.

"How far are you willing to go?" That was a loaded question, and he wasn't sure she even knew her own capacity. Knowing he was her first lover meant there were serious considerations he had to make that weren't normally in place for an experienced woman.

She thought about his question and nibbled her lip. "I guess as far as you're willing to take me." Once she said the words, she realized how true they were. She trusted him not to hurt her, and knew he had the ability to bring her great pleasure. He'd already proven that tonight.

"Oh Jessie Girl, you really shouldn't have said that." He chuckled and kissed her again. *Precious, that's what she was,* he thought. He wanted to come between her parted thighs and enjoy the sweetness of her body, but he refused to do that until she healed. Pleasurable pain might be something he enjoyed giving, but to him this was just different.

She shouldn't admit being so willing. The truth was she wanted to experience more. She didn't have enough knowledge about her own sexuality to know what more consisted of. "I trust you Chase." She spoke the truth softly, but met his eyes to let him know she meant it.

There was little a woman could say that turned him on as much as those words. He knew if he was going to keep his self-made promise to not take her again so soon, these games needed to come to an end tonight. Something about hearing those words from her lips went straight to his throbbing cock.

"I'll never let you regret that trust either Jessie. I'm going to do the right thing here and let you sleep." *Before I take your body in all the ways going through my mind right now,* he thought. With practiced ease he removed her ankle and wrist cuffs, and pulled her against his chest. "Sleep honey, we've got many more nights to explore later."

She wanted to tell him that she was willing to make love to him again, but the truth was she was still a little sore. Snuggling up against his warmth, she fell asleep with a smile on her face.

CHAPTER NINE

Sympathizing

Upon waking, she stretched languidly. She must have used several muscles she hadn't used before. Glancing around the room, she smiled, recalling the events of last night, and felt a little wicked for wishing he were in bed now so they could enjoy a few more pleasures. Sliding out of bed, she walked over to his bathroom and took a quick shower, hoping that by the time she was finished he'd be back.

Finishing her toilette, she made her way into the bedroom, disappointed he still wasn't back. Deciding she needed to find him, she pulled on her clothes and padded barefoot down the stairs. She heard someone singing in the kitchen and followed the sound. Louise was cleaning and humming a tune, and Jessie cleared her throat to let her know she wasn't alone.

"Hello, Jessie. I trust you slept well?" Louise's smiling eyes filled with warmth.

"Yes Ma'am." Jessie flushed at the thought of this kind woman knowing where she'd spent the night.

"None of that formality, dear. It's Louise. Are you hungry? I could prepare something for you." Smiling even deeper, her eyes crinkled on the sides.

"Thank you so much, Louise, but honestly I'm not really hungry. Um, do you know where Chase is?" She didn't want to offend the housekeeper, but she normally didn't eat until noon.

The sweet smile faded. "His father took a turn for the worse and they admitted him to the hospital a little after five. Chase didn't want to wake you so he asked me to let you know how sorry he was he couldn't see you home."

It was hard to be upset at his absence, knowing the reason for it. "I hope everything's all right." She knew it was a stupid response because his father was obviously dying, but she didn't know what else to say. She wished he had awakened her, but she understood his thoughts had been somewhere else.

"It will all turn out the way the good Lord intended." Louise's smile turned sad.

"I guess I should be getting home. Would you let Chase know I'm here if he needs to talk later?"

"I will, but Chase told me to let you know you could stay as long as you wished."

"Thank you, Louise, but I have some work at home to take care of. It was very nice meeting you." She wanted to walk down to the dungeon to retrieve her shoes, but had no intention of letting Louise know she'd been down there.

"Well, take care of yourself then, young lady. I hope to see you back again really soon." With a grin, she went back to cleaning.

Jessie saw her purse sitting on the coffee table where she'd left it last night, and walked over to retrieve it. Walking out the door barefoot, she shook her head before making her way to her car and driving home. It definitely wasn't how she'd expected her time with Chase to end, but then again, yesterday she'd had no idea she'd be staying the night with him, either.

Suddenly, she felt like she'd done something wrong. Pulling up in front of her apartment, she couldn't seem to shake the notion.

Unlocking her door, she reached down to pet Sebastian as he greeted her. Picking him up in her arms, she cuddled him against her chest. "Take a deep breath." Speaking to the walls, she tried to convince herself that last night was nothing to feel guilty about.

Sitting down at her small kitchen table, she put the cat down and closed her eyes. The image of Chase making love to her washed through her mind, sending a surge of desire through her body again. Without thought, her hand moved to her throat. She could easily imagine the feel of his hand there, then moving downward until he cupped her breast.

The dampness between her thighs forced her eyes open again, and she stood quickly. Confusion about wanting him again compounded with the guilty feelings she already had. Releasing a long breath, she fought back the urge to cry. She wasn't even really sure what was really upsetting her.

Needing to calm down, she picked up her phone and called Amanda. Filling her in on the barest of details, her friend agreed to stop by her apartment for lunch. She felt a little better after hanging up, but glancing down at her body, the relief dissipated. The fact that she was still wearing the clothes she'd left in yesterday reminded her of just how impulsive she'd been.

She hadn't known Chase long enough to even consider the step she'd taken last night. Not to mention, the man was dealing with some serious problems of his own at the moment, and had probably just wanted comforting. Basically, she'd thrown the promises she'd made to herself about only making love in a committed relationship out the window last night. Groaning, she hurried to her bathroom to shower.

By the time Amanda arrived, she'd worked herself into a state of melancholy. Chase hadn't called yet, and even though reasonably she knew he was probably dealing with his father, it still hurt that he hadn't picked up the phone. All her insecurities flooded over her and she broke down into tears as her best friend consoled her.

"Come on, Jessie, stop crying." Amanda hugged her tightly. "The first time is always really emotional and I promise you're making more over this than needs to be. He's probably just got his mind wrapped up in his father at the moment." Her own eyes moistened.

Jessie took a few deep breaths, knowing she was acting like a child. Mentally listing all the reasons why she was overacting helped. Pulling out of Amanda's arms, she walked over to the kitchen island bar, grabbed a paper towel, and blew her nose. "I'm sorry I'm acting like a blubbering idiot."

"No you're not, honey. You're acting like a woman who's confused about a man. I've cried on your shoulder more times than you can count on one hand."

A small smile found Jessie's face, knowing how true those words were. It still didn't make her feel less guilty. The doorbell rang and she walked over to answer it, hoping her face didn't look like a blotchy mess from all the tears. The dozen red roses that the delivery man held out almost made the waterworks start again. She signed for them quickly, and gave him a tip before walking back to the table. Picking up the card, she did start crying again. It said, *Thank you for a beautiful night I will never forget* and was signed, *Always, Chase.*

"Well, obviously someone was impressed last night." Amanda laughed softly. "At least he's thoughtful."

"Maybe he doesn't regret last night." Jessie gave a watery smile, feeling as if a weight had been lifted. She knew there was no reason to have felt like he'd been disappointed last night, but her mind had trouble accepting anyone could want her.

"Why would you think he'd regret it? I swear, sometimes I wish I could step inside that mind of yours and show you what an incredible woman you are." Anger filled her gaze, and Amanda added, "It was just sex. You did nothing wrong."

There was no way she could make Amanda understand. They thought differently. "I just wanted the first time to be with the man I planned on spending my life with."

"I swear sometimes you think out of this century." Amanda smiled sadly. "Just be happy you were with a man who obviously pleased you."

Arguing was pointless. Nodding, Jessie retrieved a vase from the kitchen, and then arranged the flowers meticulously.

Amanda changed tactics. "Let's get out of here and go shopping and stop by the hair salon."

Jessie wasn't big on the shopping idea, but she could definitely use a trim, she decided. "Okay, you're on, but I want ice cream when we're done." Feeling her spirits lift at that thought, she smiled.

The ice cream was a post-shopping tradition and Amanda grinned back. "Only if it's a double scoop of chocolate peanut butter."

Making a gagging sound, Jessie laughed again. "Personally, I don't know how you can mix chocolate and peanut butter."

They made their way down to Amanda's car and enjoyed small talk until they arrived at the mall. Jessie had convinced Amanda years ago to change from her expensive boutique to this place, since the stylist was so impressive.

By the time they left the salon and finished their shopping, all the earlier depression Jessie had felt was gone. The book club was meeting tonight, and thanks to Amanda, she had an outfit that would probably even impress some of the women there. The women all dressed in designer clothing, and that just wasn't in her conservative budget. Amanda dropped her off at her apartment, and told her they were meeting at Carolyn's house tonight.

Chase called her later in the afternoon to let her know his father was in ICU. She asked if he wanted some company but he kindly refused, saying he needed

a little time to accept things, but he did say he appreciated the offer. They talked for almost half an hour before he informed her they were letting visitors back in
and he'd call her again later. She felt much better after
their conversation, even though she wasn't completely
convinced the previous night hadn't been a mistake.

She made the conscious decision to not let any of
that affect her mood tonight. She'd even managed to
read the book this time.

CHAPTER TEN

Book Club Rule

She dressed with care in the new black sheath Amanda had helped her pick out, and the three inch heels made her feel a little more feminine. She'd even put on makeup and jewelry. When she arrived at Carolyn's house, she felt more confident than she ever had at one of these meetings.

Carolyn greeted her at the door and gave her a warm smile. "You look lovely," she said, allowing her gaze to move over Jessie.

"Thank you Carolyn. Amanda and I had a little shopping trip today." She managed to keep eye contact, something that was normally hard for her. "So how was your day?" Normally she just answered questions without adding much to a conversation.

Raising an eyebrow, Carolyn smiled warmly. "Well, I spent most of the day at Chase's club trying to familiarize myself with everything."

"Are you going to be helping him out now?" She and Chase hadn't really talked about his father last night, she remembered with a flush to her cheeks.

"Actually, I'm going to be running Sensation's, at least temporarily since Chase is taking over his father's company." Shaking her head, she sighed. "I'm not sure it's really what Chase wants, but I guess he feels like he has to make things easier on his father."

"Is he okay with that? I mean, I thought he enjoyed working at the club?" She was concerned he'd acted hastily.

Carolyn studied her intently. "I'm sure it's not easy for him. I know it's probably none of my business, but you seem really interested in Chase's feelings."

Feeling her face warm, Jessie nibbled her nip. "We um, went out the other night."

Her eyes widened. "I admit I'm somewhat shocked. I thought you'd been pretty turned off by everything that happened at Sensation's?"

Jessie's lowered her gaze and whispered. "I never said I was interested in all of that." Even as she said the words, a guilty feeling overcame her knowing she was in fact, interested.

"If Chase asked you out and you went, then I know you are." Smiling at her expression, she motioned to the living room. "Stay after the group leaves. I'd love to talk with you more."

Carolyn didn't give her time to accept or decline the offer. Walking after her into the living room, Jessie sat in her usual spot. The discussion began and for the first time since joining the book club, she felt like she had something to offer. When Carolyn asked if she thought it was possible for a dominant to be a great friend, Jessie actually gave her thoughts. "I would think a dominant would be just like any other man, and it would depend on his personality."

It was awkward when more than a few of the women looked at her with their mouths almost agape because she actually spoke. She forced a smile instead of glancing at her lap, and noticed several smiles returning to her. And a fifteen-minute conversation resulted from her comment!

After the meeting, she was shocked that a few of the women came up to talk with her, and she was even more surprised to find herself enjoying the conversation. Amanda had bailed out early, claiming she had a date with her lawyer, so after the rest of the women departed, she didn't have an excuse not to stay and talk with their host. Carolyn didn't waste any time questioning her.

"Something's different about you, Jessie." Handing her a glass of the wine, they sat down on the couch.

Taking a sip of the smooth liquid, she smiled. "This is really delicious." Not knowing exactly how to respond to her statement, she just shrugged.

"Are you and Chase playing together?" Carolyn watched her expression intently.

Jessie almost choked on her wine at the blunt question. She wondered how she should answer, then decided maybe the truth would be the best way to go. "Not really." That was true. She wasn't playing with him in the way Carolyn meant. Unless Chase tying her to the bed counted.

Taking a sip of her wine, Carolyn glanced over the glass at Jessie. "How do you 'not really' play with someone? I mean, it really is a you are or you're not situation."

A thought entered Jessie's mind. "You and Chase don't play together, do you?" Now that she'd asked the question, it really did make sense. They obviously shared the same interest, and why else would he trust her with his club?

Carolyn threw back her head back and laughed out loud. "That would never happen. I'm not a switch."

"A switch? I have no idea what a branch has to do with this."

Carolyn laughed even louder. "No, a switch is a person who enjoys being both dominant and submissive, depending on their mood. Let's just say I always like to call the shots."

Feeling her face redden, Jessie lowered her eyes in embarrassment. "Sorry. There are obviously a bunch of words in your world I haven't learned yet."

"Yet? So are you saying you are going to learn more, perhaps with Chase?"

"Seriously, I don't know at this point, Carolyn. I mean, I enjoyed staying with him last night, but as far as where it will lead, I just don't know." Realizing she'd just basically admitted sleeping with Chase, she wondered if she could be more of an idiot.

"You spent the entire night with him?" Carolyn's eyes filled with shock.

Taking a quick gulp of her wine, she wished she'd controlled her mouth filter more. "I really don't want to talk about this." That was an understatement. She'd known Carolyn for a while now, but they weren't exactly close enough to discuss this subject.

"I didn't mean to pry," Carolyn said apologetically, "I'm just worried Chase hasn't been very upfront with you about how he views relationships. He's a really nice man, but I'm not sure he's in a place to consider anyone else's needs at the moment."

That was a warning if she ever heard one, and Jessie stiffened. "I shouldn't have said anything." She already knew she'd revealed more than she should have.

Smiling encouragingly, Carolyn shook her head. "I think you're misunderstanding me. I don't want to see you get hurt. If things weren't so stressful with Chase at the moment, I'm sure he would have explained he doesn't do casual play."

Her brow wrinkled in confusion. Was the woman warning her off or telling her Chase would expect more? "I really don't understand."

"This isn't really my place, but normally Chase discusses every aspect of what he expects from a submissive before they move to the next step. From what I know of his past, women aren't invited to sleep over. His father's illness has him in a place right now where he's not thinking clearly."

"So you're saying either Chase expects me to be his submissive or he just lost his mind by sleeping with me last night?" Both those scenarios confused her, and her eyes clouded in thought.

"Honestly, I don't know what I'm saying at the moment. I just don't want you to get hurt, that's all." Standing, Carolyn walked over to the bar to refresh her wine.

Jessie couldn't help asking the question that filled her thoughts. "Why doesn't he allow women to sleep over?" The man was beautiful. She doubted seriously it was from lack of offers.

"That's something you should really discuss with Chase when his head is clear." Walking back to join Jessie on the couch, she smiled secretively.

Jessie had no idea why the gleam suddenly came into Carolyn's eyes, but she did know she was more confused than ever about what had happened between her and Chase last night. "I probably should get going. I have some work I need to catch up on before morning." The truth was, she wasn't really sure what Carolyn's intentions had been tonight and she was uncomfortable.

Nodding, Carolyn stood back up. "I'll see you out."

Walking to her car she wasn't sure what had just taken place. Carolyn seemed too curious about her relationship with Chase. Granted, she shouldn't have told her they'd been together. Driving back home she was frustrated.

CHAPTER ELEVEN

Falling Deeper

Jessie's phone was ringing as she walked in the door. With an exasperated huff, she answered. She really wanted some time to think about last night, and Carolyn's strange behavior. The interruption was annoying. But Chase's sensual voice wiped all thoughts and concerns from her mind. He sounded almost broken and the sound felt like a punch to her gut.

"I just wanted to call you back so I didn't break my word, Jessie. How was your book club meeting?"

"It was good. Are you okay, Chase? You sound, well, different..."

His voice broke as he answered. "My father passed away half an hour ago."

"Where are you, Chase? I'm coming now." She was determined he not go through this alone.

"Really, Jessie, you don't need to do that and I'm not good company at the moment. I just didn't want to make you think I'd forgotten you, so I called."

"Seriously, Chase, I want to be there for you. Just tell me where you are."

"Thank you, Jessie, but I really just need to be alone. I'll call you again tomorrow."

"Chase?" Hearing nothing but static, she knew he'd hung up on her. Thinking for a few minutes she decided on her next action.

Calling Carolyn, Jessie found out the name of the hospital Chase's father was in. Telling herself she was just making sure he wasn't in shock, she got back in her car and drove there, hoping he hadn't left. It was an impulsive move, and one she realized he might not appreciate. Deciding if he was there, he could tell her to leave after she felt assured he could drive home. She didn't allow her misgiving to change her mind.

Her heart ached when she finally saw him after getting directions from the front desk. He was sitting alone, his head buried in his arms as he wept. Jessie didn't care how inappropriate it was. She walked over and knelt before him, grabbing his hands. "Chase, I'm so very sorry. I know I can't stop the pain, but I'm here for you," she whispered soothingly while stroking his hands.

His tormented eyes met hers, and all thoughts of being the strong one evaporated at the tenderness in her actions. Wrapping his arms around her, he allowed the demeaning tears to continue. "I just thought I'd have more time with him." His voice was that of a broken man.

They remained there several moments, wrapped in each other's embrace. Jessie whispered nonsensical words attempting to soothe him, feeling his pain vibrate through her own soul. She doubted he would appreciate the stares of sympathy sent their way from other families. "Do you have any paperwork to fill out tonight?"

Shaking his head no, he tried to control himself. "There's nothing to do until tomorrow. I'll need to handle arrangements then." He almost lost it again, and tensed. Jessie's arms around him was the only thing keeping him sane.

"Then we need to get you home. I have my car here." His weak nod was all the assurance she needed to lead him out of the building. Walking hand in hand back to her car, she couldn't imagine how hard it was on this strong man to realize he couldn't stop what had happened to his father. She'd felt the same way when her own mother died

Seeing this side of him made her feel even closer to him. He allowed her to drive, and she didn't attempt to speak during the trip back to his place.

Pulling up in his driveway, she was shocked as his hand gripped hers tightly when she turned off the ignition. Lifting her eyes to him, she was stunned at the emotions filling those deep blue depths. "What is it?" she whispered, sensing he needed to ask her something.

"You'll stay with me?" *God, what was he? Six years old?* He thought as the question left his lips. Bad things happened in life. Why couldn't he just suck it up and at least put on a strong front for her?

"Of course I will." She squeezed his hand back and smiled reassuringly.

Letting out a relieved breath, he let go of her hand and opened his car door. Walking around, he opened hers and pulled her into his arms, hugging her again. After enjoying the feel of her in his arms for a moment, he released her and they walked into the house.

Louise greeted them at the front door and wrapped her arms around Chase's neck, crying loudly. "I'm so sorry Chase. Your father was a great man and I just can't believe he's gone." Releasing him, she allowed them to walk through the door. "I'll go put on a pot of coffee." Sniffling through her tears, she walked away quickly.

They walked into the den and Jessie sat down, feeling uncomfortable. There wasn't anything she could

say that was going to make this situation any easier on
him.   Losing someone you loved was never painless.
Louise bringing coffee back took away the awkward
silence.

"Louise, please sit down. You look like you're about
to fall off your feet any minute," Jessie whispered com-
passionately. She had to assume this loss hurt her as
well since Chase's father had been her employer for
many years.

Louise served them coffee, and then sat down with
them as they sipped it. Jess put her hand on Chase's
upper thigh and squeezed lightly. "I'm sorry, Chase, I
didn't know your father, but I'm sure he was a really
wonderful man." She wished she knew how to comfort
him.

"He would have loved you, Jessie." He gave her a sad
smile, knowing she was the type of woman his father
always hoped he'd settle down with.

"Yes, he would have," Louise agreed, smiling
through her tears.

Louise insisted after coffee that Chase try and get
some rest, and Jessie and he walked up to his room.
She wasn't sure what he needed from her at that moment, and watched as he undressed and climbed into
bed, feeling out of her element.

"Would you just lie with me, Jessie," he said, wanting the comfort of her arms around him. He probably

should have encouraged her to go home, but the thought of not having her here made him feel almost bereft.

Kicking off her shoes, she climbed into the bed, still clothed in her black dress. Sleeping in the outfit was probably not the best idea, but she needed to focus on him and not some stupid dress.

Pulling her into his arms as she joined him, he held her tightly. It was a strange feeling to want to lean on someone else, but oddly enough, at that moment, he didn't care. He doubted seriously he'd get any sleep tonight, but her comforting embrace soon lulled him into a strange lethargy.

The scent that was all Chase filled her pleasure. Long after his breathing leveled out, she stayed awake. When he turned on his back to sleep, she allowed her gaze to roam over his perfect physique. Wide shoulders melted into a tanned chest that was free from hair, lowering to washboard abs and his sex. She refused to let her eyes dwell on that organ of pleasure. His thighs were strong and powerful. Enjoying the view, she allowed her gaze to continue down to his muscled calves, and even his perfect feet.

Forcing her eyes back up to his beautiful, sleeping face, she wanted to trace the hard contours and memorize them so when he finally realized she wasn't good enough for him, she could dream of being here. He was pure male perfection, and her body ached in ways that overwhelmed her. Taking a deep breath, she decided sleep was the only way to escape the need.

Close to dawn, he awoke and glanced over at the beautiful woman beside him. He'd never brought a woman into his bedroom before her, and twice now she'd awakened with him. It was a feeling he was discovering he really enjoyed. Glancing over her fully clothed body, he shook his head, thinking how uncomfortable she must have been dressed this way all night while he slept like the dead.

He carefully rolled her over to her side and slid the long zipper down with ease. She moaned softly but he could tell by her breathing she was still asleep. He slid the garment from her shoulder, and then turned her over again just as gently. He worked the other shoulder strap off and managed to lower it. His mouth watered at the sight of her breasts covered by the lacy black bra that cupped her perfectly. He inched the dress down slowly. His hand moved tenderly under her hips, lifting them so he could slide it off and toss it aside.

Shivering slightly as the cool breeze moved over her body, she opened her eyes slightly and gazed up sleepily.

"Go back to sleep, honey. I was just making you comfortable." As she closed her eyes once more, he wished he had the strength of will to tear his eyes away from the perfection of her body. She was small statured, but that didn't take away anything, he decided. It just made the package more enticing. Her softly rounded hips, her perfect hand-sized breasts, even the slight bulge of her abdomen make him ache to slide between her thighs.

She wasn't fat by any means, he thought, but she definitely didn't look anorexic like the majority of other women in his life before her. He knew better than to keep looking at her, but he just couldn't seem to help himself. The soft scrap of lace covering her core was too enticing, and his fingers were drawn to trace over the outline of her plump nether lips. If her body hadn't responded, perhaps he would have been strong enough to allow her to sleep. The dampness through the thin material as he continued to rub slowly against her was more than he could resist.

Sliding under the material, he couldn't stop his finger from delving inside her warm heat. Her soft moan of pleasure encouraged him to go further. Her core was sweet perfection, he thought as he slowly withdrew. Bringing his finger to his lips, he suckled the taste of her with pleasure. He knew he should stop, but he didn't want to think about reality at the moment. He only wanted to feel what her delicious body could offer him.

Rolling over to his bedside table, he opened the drawer and found a condom. He'd bought a box of them after their last time together, vowing to never be unprepared. Sliding it over his engorged cock, he turned back to gaze over the perfection that was all Jessie. Even in her sleep, she was enchanting, he thought. Her soft lips parted as she slowly inhaled and exhaled the peace on her face making her look even more angelic. A better man would have stopped. Working the thin material of her panties down her legs, he tossed it aside, and his finger found her again.

She was having the most incredible dream, and the sensations were so real she wished she could sleep forever. Her heart felt like it was racing as a long finger slowly rode her, making her hips arch off the bed. Her body wanted more and pushed against the hand giving her such pleasure. Biting her lip, she tried not to cry out as another digit stretched her sex.

She was so wet, he thought as he parted her thighs and moved between them. Holding his cock in one hand, he pushed forward into her tightness, groaning as her flesh gripped him like a glove. Inching in slowly, he wanted to savor each sensation as she took him to her womb. Watching their bodies join was incredible, and he slowly began to move.

Her eyes opened slowly, and feeling him riding her, she almost came undone immediately. Waking from a dream to the incredible feel of him embedded so deeply in her was nothing short of amazing. Still languid, she wrapped her legs around his waist. Each slow thrust had her spiraling to the edge so quickly, she cried out his name.

Feeling her body tense, he increased the rhythm, pleased that she was enjoying how he'd awakened her. He could get used to this, he thought, watching her head fall back. Her eyes closed as she gave in to the ecstasy he was bringing her. Grabbing her wrists, placing them over her head, he never lost a stroke as he held them pinned against the mattress. His thrusts became forceful as he neared his own release, and her silken folds clenching and releasing --almost fighting against the momentum he was building-- was the closest thing to pure rapture he'd ever experienced. Grunting out her name, he had the best orgasm of his adult life.

When he could breathe again, he rolled her over on top of him. "Hell, Jessie girl, what you do to me!"

She was just as breathless as he was, and could only lie there gasping for several seconds. That was undoubtedly the most erotic lovemaking of her life, she thought. Who knew that being awakened that way could be so incredible? "I could wake up every morning like that," she said, resting her face against his chest. Realizing what she'd said, she instantly regretted the words, even if they were the truth.

He chuckled softly, allowing his hands to caress the long silky strands of hair that were now slightly damp.

"I'll remember you said that." He was shocked to feel his cock growing hard inside her again already and rolled her over before pulling out. He doubted the condom could handle another round like that, and slid out of the bed to toss it in the trash.

She watched his every movement, not sure if she should be embarrassed being sprawled out on his bed, but still so relaxed she didn't feel like moving. Chase was such an experienced lover, he'd made her feel things she'd never even dreamed possible, and when he joined her again, she felt guilty, knowing she wanted to experience even more.

"What's going on in that beautiful mind?" he asked, lowering beside her, resting on his side.

Lowering her face so as to not meet his eyes, she shook her head. She couldn't tell him what she was really thinking. He'd think she was insatiable.

"None of that shyness with me, missy." He chuckled and lifted her chin with his hand. "I truly want to know what you're thinking." He didn't add, *before I take you for another round.* Amazing as it was, his body wasn't ready to stop yet.

Nibbling on her lower lip, she decided she really didn't have anything to lose by being honest. "I was just thinking there's probably so much you could show me." She whispered the words, glad there was only a small amount of light pouring in from the now rising sun outside, so the blush she could feel on her face wasn't that visible.

As if he needed any other reason to want her, those words made him feel invincible. "Jessie girl, you may not be able to walk after I show you all the sexual pleasures I've got in store for you. Roll over on your stomach," he demanded hoarsely. The thought of all the ways he could bring her to the brink moved through his mind, and he hoped she was ready to be sore.

She didn't even think when he told her what he wanted. She turned over and waited for whatever he had in mind next. Hearing him roam around the room, she was almost impatient for him to be back in bed with her.

Sliding on another condom, he allowed his gaze to fall on her perfect, heart-shaped ass. It was more than he could resist and a hand fell against the pale flesh. He enjoyed the splash of color that immediately appeared. "Such a beautiful vision." Smiling, his large hand caressed the same spot before coming down again on the other cheek.

Tensing at the strange sensation, she realized there was little painful about what he was doing. Oddly enough, it made her ache for him. When he parted those twin globes, though, her breath caught in her throat. When his finger stroked against her untried entrance, she tensed.

"Relax, Jessie girl," he said calmly. "I promise I won't take you this way. I just want to explore." Pleased as she relaxed again, he pushed slightly against the tightness of that orifice, and inched his finger in a few inches. He knew this was something it would take months to get her comfortable enough to enjoy with him, but he was looking forward to being her first. Sliding his finger away, he lowered his mouth to find the soft petals of her sex and darted his tongue in and out until she was writhing beneath him in pleasure.

When she was ready for him, he lifted her up to rest on her elbows and slid into her from behind with unhurried movements. His finger found her other chamber, and slowly entered that untried haven. He knew she was feeling him so much deeper this way, and didn't want to rush it. "Rise up on your hands," he demanded. As soon as she complied, he used one hand to hold her hip, the other hand occupied as his finger rode her slowly.

The pleasure that soared through her at his action was unbelievable, even if the pressure of his finger was foreign. As he began to ride her, he rotated his digit, stretching her body for the way he would take her one night. He was so deep. She could feel him bumping against her womb. It was like nothing she had felt in her life before. The sensation of being filled both ways was mind blowing.

Sliding his finger from her, a moan escaped her lips that had him ready to explode.

Her body tensed and found release almost immediately as his finger pulled away. *Dear God I can't believe I feel this much*, she thought.

"I'm not done with you yet, Jessie girl. You'd better hold on." He gripped both of her hips and drove long and hard inside her, then retreated, only to plunge again. He couldn't seem to get enough, and almost didn't want to come as his own body exploded. His mind wasn't ready to stop yet, so his fingers stroked her until she fell apart at the seams. Pulling from her clenching flesh, he wondered how many times he could help her find paradise. Allowing his thumb to push inside her drenched core, he was determined to find out.

Moving his thumb back to her tight orifice, he pushed inside, the lubrication making it much easier this time. Sliding in and out, he noted she was not resisting him at all and smiled. "Can you come again, Jessie girl? Shall we see?"

"I can't, Chase," she whimpered softly. Her body had never known so much pleasure and she wasn't sure if she could handle any more.

"I bet you can, Jessie girl." He chuckled wickedly, allowing his other hand to move around to the front. His thumb slowly rode her untried chamber. With his other hand, he allowed two fingers to pinch her clit.

"Come for me, Jessie. Don't deny me." He was exhausted but refused to give up this battle.

She wanted to beg him stop, even as her body screamed for even more. The sensation of having him touch her this way was almost too much. "Chase, please," she cried out as her body tensed yet again on the brink of fulfillment. *Surely she would die from all these incredible sensations*, she thought.

He wasn't giving in and rode her faster with his thumb. Allowing the other two fingers to slide into her core, he plunged deeply. He knew she was capable of great passion. She just needed someone to bring it out in her. "Come now, Jessie girl!" He raised his voice as his fingers continued to crescendo, playing her body expertly until she cried out in completion. "That's my sweet girl," he cooed. Pulling his fingers from her flesh, he turned her over, allowing her to fall back on the bed. Pulling her into his arms, he held her tightly.

They both fell asleep again, and he woke her later, demanding all her body would give and then more. When he knew he had to leave the bed, it was with a sense of regret. His mind had been on pleasing her, and doing so had pushed all his other worries to the backburner. He knew that sooner rather than later he had to face reality though, and he wasn't a man that hid from the truth.

"Grab a shower, sweet girl, and I'll go ask Louise to get breakfast started." Giving her a tender smile and a chaste kiss on her lips, he slid out of bed, found his shorts and left her alone in the room.

CHAPTER TWELVE

Light of Day

Making her way into his bathroom, there was no doubt about how sore she was. Her muscles ached in ways they'd never known before and she giggled. Thinking she now knew what it meant to be truly sexually satisfied. Standing under the warm spray of the shower, she didn't laugh at the stinging sensation between her thighs. The man was insatiable, she thought with a grin as she washed off. If she was able to walk today, it was going to be a miracle.

Stepping out of the shower, she realized she didn't have any regrets about what had happened last night. While Chase might have been insatiable, he was also a very generous lover, and there was no denying how much pleasure he'd given her. The ache between her thighs was definitely a small price to pay.

Walking back into his room, she didn't want to slide on her dress again and meet Louise. Without thinking twice, she went through his drawers and found a t-shirt and a pair of shorts that were entirely too big, but she rolled them down at the waist until she was assured they wouldn't fall off. She looked like a child playing in adult clothes, she decided, and laughed at her appearance in the full-sized mirror on his door.

No help for it. She shrugged and walked downstairs to find Chase, still barefoot. She was shocked as she noticed the time on the elegant clock hanging on the wall. It was already after twelve in the afternoon. Had they really been enjoying each other that long? Making her way to the kitchen, she smiled, seeing Louise, and tried to hide a blush.

"Well, hello there young lady." Louise smiled warmly. "I'm almost done here if you want to join Chase in the dining room." She pointed to the room behind her.

"Thank you, Louise, and good morning," she said, hurrying off to the other room, knowing it wasn't morning at all. Chase was talking on his cell phone, and she could tell the conversation wasn't a pleasant one. Sitting down at the imposing dining room table, she kept quiet while he continued his conversation.

He gave her a slight smile as he spoke with Carolyn, not wanting her to think he was upset with her. He wished he could go back to their fantasy land back in the bedroom. "Sorry," he mouthed as he listened to Carolyn. Louise had contacted his friend early this morning and she was helping to make funeral preparations.

Jessie shook her head to indicate he shouldn't be sorry, and smiled as Louise came in with a coffee tray. She poured them both a cup and asked quietly what she took. Jessie kept her tone low as she whispered, "Cream and sugar."

Chase hung up with a loud sigh, putting the phone down on the table. "Morning." He forced a wink and a smile he didn't feel at the moment, but he wanted her to be comfortable.

"Afternoon," she whispered with a sad smile, knowing exactly what he was doing. "Are you okay?"

He nodded curtly, knowing he wasn't fooling her. "Carolyn was just giving me all the details for my father's funeral. Thank you Louise." He gave a half smile as she put his cup before him.

"I'll be back in with your breakfast." Louise nodded and walked back to the kitchen.

"I know how hard this is for you, Chase. If you need some time alone, I'll understand." She had enjoyed the most beautiful experience of her life last night, but she didn't want to feel like she was imposing on him during his time of grief.

He didn't want her to deal with the grief he was feeling, and nodded. "I probably could use a little time to myself Jessie, but let's eat our breakfast first, okay?" He didn't want her to leave, but it really wasn't right to ask her to stay again.

She was more than a little disappointed, but understood. Forcing a smile, she nodded. They ate their breakfast in relative silence before she stood to excuse herself. "Call me later if you feel up to it." She managed a fake smile. She didn't want him to think she was upset about his decision.

"I wish we had met at a better time," he said, smiling apologetically. He walked her to the car, though he didn't want to let her leave. But she'd already done so much for him.

Reigning in her emotions at his words, she gave another brave smile. His kiss on her cheek seemed like a forever goodbye, and it was breaking her heart. She managed to slide into her car and drive off before the waterworks started.

Pulling off on the side of the road after she'd driven a few blocks, she allowed the tears to fall. Carolyn had warned her that he wasn't in the right frame of mind for a relationship. She herself knew how she'd reacted after her own mother passed away. None of that make the aching hurt less.

When she felt composed enough to drive, she headed back to her apartment. She wasn't that woman who could just casually sleep with a man. Granted, she hadn't known Chase very long, but already she felt things for him that surpassed anything she'd felt for Greg.

But she understood what he was going through. Jessie walked through her front door and tossed down her purse. She realized that while he probably did like her and felt attracted to her, he had needed to be comforted and she'd been available. The thought didn't sit well in her mind.

Pulling out her phone, she checked her messages, attempting to find something that would take her mind off the emotions that kept building. Seeing Amanda's text, her heart nearly stopped.

"I need you to call me. Where are you? Damn it, this is important." Reading Amanda's words, her own misery receded and she dialed her friend's number. Amanda finally answered after the fifth ring.

"Are you okay?" Jessie asked anxiously.

"No I'm not. I've been trying to call you all night. Please come over to my place." Amanda spoke the words in a rush.

Grabbing her purse again, Jessie talked as she made her way back to the car. "You're starting to scare me here. What's going on?"

"Just get here, and I'll explain." Amanda cried.

"I'm driving now. Do I need to call someone?" Jessie had no idea what was going on, and she floored the accelerator. Thankfully, Amanda only lived a few miles away, and she could get to her condo quickly.

"No!" Amanda screamed.

Hearing the panic in her friend's voice, Jessie's own hands trembled. Amanda was completely freaked out and not acting like herself. "I'm almost there now."

Getting silence on the other end, Jessie was close to panicking herself. After pulling up in front of the building, she took off running toward the elevator. Tapping her foot impatiently, she mentally urged the thing to come faster. Standing in front of her friend's door a couple minutes later, she knocked soundly.

Amanda pulled her into her arms and whimpered. "I don't know what to do." Tears fell down her cheeks.

Jessie forced herself out of the death grip Amanda had around her neck, and gasped as she saw the bruise on her cheek. "What happened?" Her eyes widened even more as she noted the ripped clothing her friend wore.

"He wouldn't stop." She paced the room, wincing with every step.

"Who wouldn't stop? You need a doctor!" She could see the pain Amanda was in, and her mind was completely overwhelmed. Who would hurt her, and why hadn't she called an ambulance?

"Derrick, the stupid prick lawyer," she said, sobbing."I can't go to the hospital. Everyone will know what he did."

"He hurt you." Judging from the bruise alone, the prick needed to be in jail. "You can't let him get away with this!" Jessie walked over to the phone and picked it up, determined that if her friend wouldn't report him, she definitely would.

Moving fast, Amanda grabbed the phone out of her friend's hand and slammed it down. "No, Jessie, my dad will find out. It was my stupidity. I shouldn't have let him tie me up."

Jessie's mouth fell open as the implications of what Amanda was saying hit home. "He beat you?" The bruise on her face was bad enough, but obviously it had gone even further.

"I just don't want to be alone. Could you please just sit with me? I'm afraid he'll come back." Forcing her legs to move her back to the couch, she sat down, her face skewed with agony.

"If you won't let me call the police, at least let me call Carolyn." It wasn't the solution she wanted, but maybe she would be able to talk some sense into Amanda.

Amanda's defeated nod was all the encouragement she needed, and she picked up the phone again. After giving Carolyn a brief description of what was happening and asking her to come over, she rejoined her friend on the couch.

"How badly are you hurt?" Jessie asked If the injuries were serious, she was calling an ambulance, whether Amanda liked it or not.

With a grimace, Amanda lifted her shirt, showing off the red whelps across her abdomen, thighs, and breasts.

Jessie covered her mouth in horror. She couldn't believe someone could do something like this. The wounds didn't seem life-threatening, but she could imagine how painful they were. "Oh my God, what kind of monster would do that?" Her own eyes filled with tears, and she hugged her friend gingerly, mindful of her pain.

"He seemed like such a nice guy, but he went crazy the minute he tied me to the bed." Sobbing, she recounted to Jessie how he'd taken a cane he claimed he'd just bought, and while telling her what a dirty whore she was, he'd beaten her body without remorse.

Jessie was disgusted, and felt bile rising up in her throat. The doorbell rang, and watching her friend tense in fear, she wished the man was here so she could tie up his ass and torture him. "I'm sure it's just Carolyn." Forcing a smile to her face, she walked over and looked through the peephole before letting her in.

Amanda told the story again, and Carolyn was just as angry as Jessie had been. She continued to encourage her to call the police, and not let the man get away with what he'd done. Frustrated that Amanda wouldn't budge, she got Jessie to help her change her clothes and settle her in bed. Giving her a pain pill from her own stash, they sat with her for the rest of the afternoon.

Amanda finally agreed to go stay at Carolyn's house for a few days until they were sure the jerk-off lawyer wouldn't come around again. His name would be blacklisted at the club, and Carolyn said she'd give his name to every group she knew in the area to make sure the man never abused anyone like this again.

Jessie drove back to her own apartment as they headed to Carolyn's, feeling nauseated at the thought of someone hurting her friend that badly. She hadn't mentioned it to either of them, but she couldn't stop the thought that none of this would have happened if they hadn't got mixed up in Carolyn's crazy lifestyle.

The next morning she received flowers from Chase, but she tossed them in the trash can. She knew he was probably just thanking her for sleeping with him, so it made her feel a little dirty, not to mention she wasn't in the best frame of mind to think about the things he enjoyed at the moment.

Another day went by and her self-confidence was in the toilet. On the one hand, she was glad Chase hadn't called because she wasn't sure she'd ever feel safe around people like him again. On the other hand, it drove home the fact that he'd only been using her for comfort. Neither thought said much about him. The only positive news was that Amanda had finally broken down and called the police.

The prick of a lawyer was charged with assault and Amanda moved in with Carolyn until his court date. She needed to get out of this place, Jessie told Sebastian as he curled up in her lap. A good long break away from everything here might help her get her head on straight again. Working like crazy hadn't stopped the thoughts pounding through her mind, so maybe a change of scenery would. It had been a week, but felt like months since Amanda's attack.

Making the decision, she called work, explaining she'd be out of town for a week. Jessie told them she wouldn't be available if something came up that required her being there in person.

She called Amanda and let her know she was taking a trip down to Florida. Amanda had asked if she wanted company, but she told her she needed some time to regroup. She gave her the hotel information, but asked her to keep it to herself. She had no doubt the company would drive her crazy with technical help questions if she didn't, even though this was her first vacation since she had started working there. *Working vacation*, she reminded herself, but still, it was a chance to get away.

After packing up her car and Sebastian, she set out. Soon enough, the greenery turned into white sandy beaches and palm trees. She rolled down the windows and inhaled the salty air. Finally pulling up to her hotel, she checked in at the front desk, and then unloaded her bags. The beach was calling her name, but she wanted to get all her things arranged first. Half an hour later, Sebastian was curled up sleeping, and she finally made it down to the sugary sand and took a deep breath.

Tossing out her beach towel, she sat down and pulled out a book. Getting lost in the pages of someone else's romance for a few hours, she found relief. That relief was short lived when she realized she'd forgotten sunscreen. She knew she'd be suffering the effects of her forgetfulness the rest of the night. At least the characters in her books had their acts together, she thought. Chuckling wryly she packed up and bypassed the hotel in favor of the local drugstore.

Picking up a bottle of ibuprofen and aloe-vera, she decided to walk around before heading back to the room. May was already tourist season, and everywhere she looked there were couples or college kids enjoying their surroundings. A couple of whistles from younger men who'd enjoyed a little too much alcohol didn't faze her. Ignoring them, she stopped in at several shops and picked up a few little items to remind her of the trip, and a few new toys for her pet. She was enjoying acting like a tourist.

For the rest of the week, she refused to let her mind settle on Chase. She did her work at night, and kept herself busy during the day shopping, or just enjoying the beach. She didn't forget sunscreen again, since the first two days of her trip were almost miserable because of her forgetfulness. The only time she couldn't escape him was in her dreams, and in those, he was the most beautiful lover a woman could imagine. She awoke several nights with tears in her eyes.

Checking out of her hotel after packing up, she felt the vacation had definitely been something she needed. Even though she missed him, there was a part of her that knew she could handle going back to the city again. She even managed to smile as the long road stretched out before her and she listened to some of her favorite songs on the radio. Then *that* song came on the radio. It reminded her so much of Chase, that she almost had to stop the car. The song discussed a woman who was always failing in love, and it really hit home. A few deep breaths later, she relaxed again, continuing to drive.

CHAPTER THIRTEEN

Wrath of Lovers

Chase was beyond frustrated after a week of trying to contact Jessie and being thwarted at every turn. He had called to ask her out the day after his father's funeral, even if it seemed a little wrong to do something like that. Reaching her voice mail time and time again, he finally badgered Carolyn to find out where she'd gone. He felt a little like a stalker as he discovered she'd went on vacation.

The thoughts going through his mind had not been pleasant. He imagined her on the beach with some new lover, and he almost gave into the temptation to drive down and drag her back home. Some part of him had already decided she was his. Forcing himself not to act like the alpha male he was, he decided to wait until she returned before demanding she tell him to his face she wasn't interested.

Carolyn had called to inform him she'd be returning today and he was on edge as he picked up the phone again for the fifth time to call her. He knew he was being irrational, but he felt almost used and discarded and it hurt his ego. When she picked up the phone, it took everything he had not to tell her just how aggravated he was. "Hello, Jessie." He spoke the words calmly, and wished he felt that way.

Hearing his voice on the other end of the line made her heart race until she remembered he was the reason she'd left in the first place. "Hello, Chase. How are you?" She didn't want him to know how hard it had been to forget his face, and could only assume he was calling out of courtesy.

"Did you enjoy your trip?" He asked, ignoring her question. He wanted to demand to know if she was sleeping with someone else, but doubted that conversation would come out any way but possessive-sounding on his end.

"Um, yeah, I enjoyed the break." How did he even know she'd been gone, she wondered? Then considered Carolyn must have talked to Amanda. "How are things going with you?" This conversation needed to end. It almost sounded like he cared, and she couldn't let herself believe that.

"I'm okay but I didn't call to talk about me. Would you like to have dinner tonight?" He wanted to see her face. He wasn't a saint by any means, but after learning what her friend had gone through at the hands of a brute, he was really worried she was putting him in the same category.

"I don't think that's such a good idea, Chase." She wanted to say yes, but dinner with him would only end in two ways, and both would hurt eventually. She couldn't imagine just having a polite conversation with him, and if they ended up in bed, she knew it wouldn't mean the same thing to him as it did to her. A week wasn't long enough to forget how Amanda's experience with a man in the lifestyle had ended up.

"And why not, Jessie girl? Did you not enjoy our nights together?" If she wasn't going to meet him, then he at least wanted to hear the truth from her lips.

Flushing, she felt her heart race even more. "I think you know I did, Chase, but we just seem to want different things." She wasn't going to say he'd just been using her to not deal with his pain, even though it really felt that way. He'd been dealing with a tough situation, and maybe if the roles were reversed she'd have done the same. She doubted it, though. Sex obviously meant a lot more to her.

"Maybe you should come over and discuss the things you want, Jessie. I can't please you if I don't know what you want." He was more than a little disappointed, and frustrated that just when he'd initiated her into the world of lovemaking, Amanda's situation had turned her completely off his lifestyle.

The thought of being with him again that way made her libido skyrocket, but how could she give herself to a man who would never see her as more than a object of sexual gratification? *At least you'd enjoy yourself,* her subconscious argued. *Right up until the moment he decided to turn into psycho man,* her mind answered back. "Is that what you really want Chase, someone to enjoy passionate games with?"

"I guess the real question here is what do *you* really want? We obviously have good chemistry, Jessie. Why shouldn't we enjoy each other?" He didn't want her to walk away. There were so many things he wanted to share with her. But all of them involved her trusting him.

"I'm sure Carolyn explained what happened to Amanda. I'm not sure I'll ever feel comfortable playing in your world again," she admitted finally. That was only part of the problem. Even if she could trust him in that capacity, he would never want the type of relationship she craved with him.

Running a weary hand through his thick hair, he sighed. "That man wasn't a master. He was barely a human being. Surely you don't put me on that same level?"

"I don't think you're that type of person, but I admit I'm a little leery of the thought of being hurt that way." A little was an understatement. She wasn't sure she'd ever recover from abuse like that.

"Any woman would be, but that's not really the question. Do you think I would hurt you like that?" If she thought he could be that sadistic, then there was no hope for them at all.

She thought about his question deeply and shook her head. "No, I know you wouldn't do something like that." She meant it. No matter how insensitive he was to her feelings for him, he wasn't the type of man to abuse another woman. That much she knew for certain.

Releasing the breath he'd been holding waiting for her answer, he relaxed somewhat. "Come see me tonight then. I really would like to talk to you."

She knew talking would turn into something else if she visited him. But would it be so horrible to enjoy him as a lover, knowing it would never go any further? Could she be that woman who just enjoyed the sensual side of her nature? Maybe that was the only way she'd get over the urge to want more than just pleasure with him. "We both know it would end in more than talking." At least that was honest, even if she hated saying the words out loud.

He wasn't going to deny that. "The choice is yours, Jessie. It always has been. If you're still interested, stop by my house tonight at eight." He hung up, not giving her time to answer; afraid he would beg her to give him a chance. If she came tonight, he would introduce her into the real world of domination, and if she didn't, he had to accept that she just didn't want him.

Listening to the dial tone for several seconds, she finally hung up. It hurt to know she'd been right and he'd only wanted to be with her to fulfill his needs. He didn't really want to talk, she decided. He wanted to enjoy her. It hurt knowing that was what he really cared about.

The hurt finally blended into anger. Two could play at his game, she decided, even knowing she would be the one that would pay the price when it all ended. She'd fought against her sexuality for years, and he was the first man to awaken her to desire. Why shouldn't she enjoy herself, if only for short time? It went against everything she believed about herself, but for once she just didn't care.

Unpacking her suitcases, she arranged everything meticulously as she thought over her options. It was obvious that she still wanted the man, even if these weren't exactly the terms she wanted him on. At least she would hopefully have a few months of memories to take away with her when this was over. Her decision already made, she took a long, hot bath, and soaked to clear her head.

She dressed to please him. Knowing that at least he found her sexually appealing did more than she'd thought possible for her self-confidence. Pulling a never-worn, slinky red dress from her closet, she slid it over her head, pleased it still fit after years of hanging abandoned. The silky little garment had been one she bought when her ex had planned to take her out dancing, before he'd broken the news about his new relationship. It somehow seemed fitting to wear this for Chase tonight.

A shrink would have a field day with her thoughts at the moment, she thought as she prepared herself to give her body to a man who obviously couldn't love her. Knowing the types of things he enjoyed, she hoped her heart was the only thing that came out of this broken. She instantly berated herself for that thought. She knew Chase would never physically hurt her.

Driving to his house, she attempted to talk herself out of this madness. She almost turned around several times, but minutes later she found herself in his driveway. "This has got to be the stupidest thing you've ever done, Jess," she said out loud as she climbed out of the car. Walking up to his door, her knees trembled in anticipation of facing him. Louise's smiling face met her instead.

"It's good to see you, young lady. You've been missed around here." Patting Jessie's hand affectionately, Louise opened the door so she could enter.

"It's nice to see you, Louise." The other woman's smile was infectious and she returned it while squeezing her hand gently.

"Chase is waiting for you in his study. You go on up and I'll bring some drinks." Pointing to the stairs, she walked off.

Forcing her legs to move, Jessie walked upstairs and followed the hall until she saw the open door of the study. Giving Chase a timid smile, she gazed over him as he sat behind the large mahogany desk. "Evening," she whispered softly.

"I'm glad you came, Jessie." He gave a forced smile and encouraged her to sit down in the oversized chair in front of the desk with a hand motion.

He didn't seem as warm and affectionate as she remembered, and an uncomfortable feeling moved through her. For a reason she couldn't explain, he seemed almost angry. "Did you change your mind?" That was the only explanation that made sense to her.

"Why on earth would I do that? We enjoy each other. There's no reason that we shouldn't continue to do so." Sensing that she didn't truly believe him, he sighed deeply. He needed to get his emotions under control. He wanted more than just some sexual rendezvous, he realized. "I just want to discuss some details before we decide where we want to go here, Jessie. I'm sorry if I seem a little tense."

This was how he normally treated the submissive's interested in training with him. He'd done things wrong with her from the beginning, but tonight he was determined to show her how he acted when he kept his emotions out of the equation. What he really wanted to do was pull her into his arms and demand that she want more from him that just the sexual pleasure he gave, but that wasn't going to happen. He felt like the woman in a relationship needing emotional depth, and it pissed him off.

They were interrupted by Louise bringing in a tray with a bottle of wine and long-stemmed glasses. They both thanked her and the silence when she left again was a little daunting to Jessie.

"I guess the best way to begin is to explain what I'm looking for in a submissive." That was who he was; he didn't see any reason to sugarcoat what his needs were. If he could have her as something more, he would have worked into this as their relationship progressed, but that wasn't the case now.

Who is this man? She thought to herself as she nodded for him to continue. He seemed almost business-like at the moment, and she wasn't sure that a relationship like this was something she could do.

"You've already been introduced to my dungeon, so you know the toys and such I like to play with. I explained before if you belonged to me, when you enter it should always be undressed and ready to please me." This felt so cold and calculated, but the thought of playing with her there still excited him, so if this is what she wanted, he had no problem giving it to her.

"You know I don't have a real grasp on the things you enjoy, Chase." Was she really going to do this with him? It wasn't what she wanted; she wanted that sweet man who loved her body so tenderly back again.

"You'll learn as I teach you, so that's not really an issue. If you aren't comfortable with something, you can just ask me to stop. I'm not going to get into details about safe words and such until I know your limits better. I'm not big on the sir and master titles either. Respect is something you show in actions, not in words, so you can continue to call me Chase."

She hadn't even considered calling him anything other than his given name, and wondered if she would have been able to do it if he'd demanded it. "Okay." She didn't like this coolness at all and wished he'd just take her in his arms again. None of this seemed right.

"I will be training you as a submissive, so I will use punishment, but I promise it won't be unbearable."

The punishment thing terrified her. "I think you'd better explain." After seeing what Amanda went through, she wasn't willing to trust even him without knowing more.

He knew automatically where her mind had gone. "Do you really think I would hurt you the way Amanda was?"

"No, but I also know you're acting strange and I'm not comfortable with you at the moment." Being honest with him seemed only right.

Running a hand through his hair, he sighed. "I just want to make sure we understand each other, I'm sorry if I seem abrupt." Softening his countenance, he smiled. "You have my word that I would never push you further than you can accept, okay?"

She nodded, but wasn't sure having him punish her was something she wanted to consider. She didn't know what she could do that would disappoint him enough to encourage that. She didn't know what to say, and again she questioned her sanity for wanting to share any part of him he was willing to give. It really was pathetic, she decided.

"Are you sure this is what you really want?" He didn't feel much like a dominant at the moment. Having her in his bedroom was much more along the lines of what he sought.

Run, her mind screamed in warning. This wasn't what she'd come for tonight, so why was she nodding? "I want to learn more about your world." She wasn't ready at all. Allowing him to use her as a sex toy seemed so callous. This all felt so impersonal, and she suddenly doubted she could make it through even one night with him as her master.

He stood. He could do this, he reminded himself. This was a role he'd played many times before. It didn't matter if he wanted more. He could give her what she needed and take what she willingly gave.

She followed him to the door leading to the basement, and felt a little nauseated at the thought of what she was going to allow tonight. The man she'd fantasized about was a complete stranger compared to this no-nonsense man leading her into a world of sexual deviance.

"You can change over there." He pointed to a small curtained area in the corner of the room, determined to keep his emotions in check. His body would find pleasure, but he'd be damned if he let his heart get any more involved.

Taking his direction, she walked behind the screen and stood several seconds before beginning to undress. She could still change her mind, she told herself, even as her fingers released her bra and allowed it to slide silently to the floor. Crossing her arms over her breasts when she was completely nude, she took several more seconds to mentally argue about this foolish endeavor.

When she walked out from behind the curtain, his breath caught in his throat at the loveliness of the vision before him. She trembled as she made her way to him. He had never wanted a woman more in his life. He could read how nervous she was, and made the decision that no matter what happened he would make sure she enjoyed herself tonight. If this was all he could have, then he would leave her with memories she would think of long after he was gone.

"My beautiful Jessie girl." Giving his first real smile of the evening, he allowed his eyes to roam over her trembling form. Making her comfortable in her own skin was the first lesson he would teach her. "Walk across the room for me," he demanded softly. As she began walking, he issued several orders. "Pull your shoulders back, keep your head up, and be proud of the beautiful body you're displaying."

After a few minutes of walking back and forth, the embarrassment left her. Placing her hands on her hips, she stopped and glanced at him. "Do you like making me walk?"

Chuckling at her response, he nodded. "I love watching you move, Jessie. It turns me on."

She couldn't argue with that compliment. She began walking again. Knowing he was watching her was somewhat of a turn-on, even if she wanted to cover herself. She had never felt this comfortable nude, even in the shower stalls at the gym.

"Walk to me, Jessie girl." He held out his arms, and smiled as she pressed against him. He allowed his arms to hold her tightly as he stroked her hair. "You look beautiful fully undressed," he whispered.

The compliment stroked her ego, even if she disagreed, but she was glad he found her worthy. The feel of his arms around her was incredible, and she snuggled against him more tightly. Pressing her lips against his chest where his shirt was opened, she inhaled the scent of him deeply, pleased.

He led her through kneels next, and enjoyed the site of her exquisite form as she surrendered to his training. She was very graceful, and after several tries, each kneel looked as if she'd practiced many times before. She was pleased to see he was aroused at the site of her own willingness to please him.

"You're almost a natural at this Jessie," he said, smiling encouragingly. The thoughts of the last week vanished as he relaxed into the role he'd been born to play. Taking her hand, he led her over to the cross. "I've dreamed of seeing you splayed up here, willing to do whatever I asked."

She'd had her own dreams about him since first tethering him to the cross at his club, and smiled. "I have a fondness for this as well."

Grinning wickedly, he attached her wrists and ankles to the cuffs that were embedded in the wood with a secure latch, then stood back to admire her body. "That first night we met, I wanted to do things like this to you." He trailed his hand from her collarbone to her breast, lifted the slight weight, and ran his finger across the coral peak, enjoying how it immediately tightened.

He had thought about her that way even then? A pleased smile found her face, making her forget everything but the sensations she was experiencing at that moment. Knowing this beautiful man wanted her was more than she could have ever wished for. Closing her eyes, she gave in to the delicious feeling of his hand fondling her.

Stepping away, he walked over to his toy chest and pulled out clamps that were connected to a thin silver chain. Moving in front of her, he fondled her breasts for several seconds until her nipples were stiff enough to accept the small little toy. These didn't add much pressure, he thought, and the sensation should be one she'd enjoy. Her soft gasp of pleasure as he attached them proved his thoughts correct.

Tugging lightly on the chain connected to her nipples, he smiled as her neck arched back and her eyes closed. Trailing his hand down through the small downy curls, he tugged slightly. "I'm going to remove these curls the next time you're here." Sliding his finger against the hard nub at her core, he continued caressing her until she was moaning softly. He attached the last clamp to her clit, and a gasp left her lips.

"Chase," she called out at the almost blinding pleasure that seeped through her body. It was almost too much, but not quite enough.

"Do you want me to remove it, Jessie girl?" He smiled, reading the confusion in her eyes. He doubted the clamp was painful enough to make her uncomfortable, but it was a sensation that took getting used to.

She shook her head no, and bit her lip, still shocked at the need the device sent raging through her core. When he tugged gently, she almost came undone. "Oh, God!"

He chuckled softly, enjoying her response, and stood back to watch her. She discovered quickly that even the slightest movement of her body pulled on the clamps since they were all attached. "Ready for more?"

How was she supposed to answer that? She wondered. The clamps had her very aware of her own body and that was definitely something she wasn't used to. "Maybe?"

He chuckled again at her answer, thinking what a joy she was to train. Walking over to his box of pleasures, he pulled out a mini-flogger. He would try a full-sized one on her at a later time, but for now he was enjoying the clamps. Moving in front of her body, he allowed the small hand-sized leather straps to gently fall over her abdomen.

Her movement increased the pressure pulling on the clamps again, and she moaned softly. Wanting this to be pure pleasure for her tonight, he began lightly flogging her with the small flogger until she was crying out. The clamps pulling at her nipples and sex, combined with the texture of the leather on her skin seemed to be something she truly enjoyed. After long moments of teasing her this way, he tossed the flogger aside and carefully undid the clamps one by one.

She was breathless by the time they were all removed, and the slight throbbing of her nipples and clit again had her completely focused on her body. When he released her from the cuffs, she wanted to demand he make love to her. She forced herself to wait for him to make that move.

Knowing what she needed was part of being a good dominant, but she had to earn what she wanted. "Pleasure me, Jessie girl," he demanded softly, encouraging her to find her knees with a slight pressure on her shoulder from his hand.

The fact that she didn't know crap about pleasing a man that way didn't matter at the moment. She wanted to please him. Unzipping his pants, she slid them awkwardly down his legs, and his underwear followed. Faced with his impressive shaft, she wrapped her hand around the width, and squeezed before taking him slowly into her mouth.

She'd thought tasting a man this way would not be as sexy as they made it in books, but she discovered immediately that she loved it. Going on her own instincts, she stroked him as she took him deeper within the confines of her mouth. The rhythm was almost natural as she relaxed her throat, allowing him to move even deeper.

"Damn, Jessie girl," he said, shaking his head. He tangled his hands in her long silken tresses, trying his best not to force his cock down her throat. She was unbelievable; he thought as he forgot for a moment and pulled her against him, forcing his impressive length down her throat. Her small gag reminded him that this was new to her and he immediately relaxed the hands fisted in her hair, letting her find her own pace again.

Rolling her tongue over his engorged head seemed to make him tense, and she assumed it was in pleasure, so she continued doing it each time she released him from her mouth. Closing her eyes, she gave herself over to the delight of pleasing him.

She definitely wasn't ready to have him take her mouth the way he truly wanted, although she was doing one hell of a job at the moment. Pulling away, he took a few deep breaths. "I think we'll practice letting me fill your mouth another time, Jessie girl. For now, I want you on that table with your gorgeous little legs spread!"

The command he gave should have embarrassed her, but she was so turned on from pleasing him, that she didn't even think as she followed his command. Lying on the table, she tried to calm her racing heart. When he demanded she spread her thighs, any hope of that happening failed.

He didn't wait for her to comply. His hands moved between her thighs and parted them quickly before moving under her ass to lift her as his tongue found her core. He feasted on the sensual treat until he felt her tense. "Keep those legs spread!"

Kicking off his shoes, he reached for his wallet, pulling a condom out. Rolling it down his length, he moved between her parted thighs, raising her by the hips and pulling her to the edge before driving home in one forceful thrust.

She didn't have time to think as he drove into her like a man starved for sex. Clinging to him, she could barely breathe as he rode her hard and quick. Each stroke had her barreling toward paradise and her body clenched and released, begging for him to take her over the edge. "Please, Chase," she cried out, needing him with a desire that couldn't be put into words.

"Come now, Jessie!" He shouted the words and continued the pounding rhythm until she tensed around his cock, holding him like a vice as her body flooded with her passion. He came just as quickly, and for a brief second, pinpoints of light took over his vision. "Damn." Having her this way was obviously something his body had wanted because he'd never had a release like that in all his adult years.

She attempted to catch her breath, amazed that she'd enjoyed the raw sensuality he'd unleashed tonight. When she thought about a dream lover, it had never been in a situation like this, even after all the BDSM books. But she knew her fantasies would be centered on scenarios like this from now on.

His world came back into focus, and the beautiful woman underneath him made his heart ache as he remembered how fully she'd submitted to him tonight. This was someone he could cherish. He'd never truly understood what that word meant until this very moment. All the sexual gratification he'd experienced with countless other submissive's paled in comparison to the exquisite emotional bond he had with this one small slip of woman.

Lifting her hand to stroke his cheek, she smiled languidly, still enjoying the aftermath of being loved so well. Still embedded deeply, she realized that being connected with him this way was more than just a physical fulfillment. Maybe her own inexperience was clouding the truth, but she couldn't imagine two people sharing such an incredible union without the heart being involved as well.

Remembering why she was here, he slid from her flesh, and tried to contain his emotions. Picking up his discarded clothes, he dressed quickly, not glancing back until the task was completed. "You pleased me well tonight, Jessie girl." The words came out harshly as he fought to hide the emotions he longed to share with her.

The reality of his words sank home, and she slid from the table, feeling ashamed at what they'd just done. Obviously, she was the only one who had felt emotionally connected as they'd made love tonight. Chiding herself mentally for allowing herself to call what they did making love, she amended the term to 'screwed'. Which was what she was at the moment: one-hundred percent screwed. Wanting to be as callous as he had been with his words, she retorted, "Glad I could be of service."

He watched as she stomped back toward the dressing curtain, completely perplexed by the anger in her words. He'd given her what she obviously needed, so why did she seem ready to kick him in the nuts instead of pleased by the compliment he'd given her? When she returned, fully dressed, he was still trying to understand what he'd done wrong tonight. There was no way she hadn't enjoyed it: her body's response had been vivid proof of that. He certainly wasn't prepared for the words she threw at him next.

"I'm sure this is how you enjoy getting your rocks off, Chase, but I can't do this. I thought I could, but I'm not this person." Never in her life had she been this emotional, not even when her ex had confessed he was a closet homosexual. "You might be great in bed, but if that's all you have to offer, then I'm just not interested." After her much needed outburst, she stormed from the room, glad that for once in her life she'd spoken her mind.

His mouth hung open for a few seconds, and he stood rooted to the spot in stunned silence. What the hell was she talking about? She was the one who was looking for someone to fulfill her sexual cravings; he wanted more. The woman obviously had no damn idea what she wanted. He marched after her, finally realizing she was leaving before they had a chance to discuss what happened tonight.

She didn't slow down her pace as she made her way back to the car. What the hell had she been thinking? She derided herself. She wasn't the type of woman who could have casual sex with a man and be all right with it. And what they'd done was even more than that. What kind of sick, twisted mentality made a man want to dominate a woman and who was she that she'd actually enjoyed the perverse pleasure he'd shown her tonight? Opening her door angrily, she had one idea in mind: Get the hell out of here and never return again.

He grabbed her arm as she was about to get in the car, without thinking of anything other than not allowing her to leave this way. "Jessie, we need to talk about what happened here tonight." He kept his voice calm, knowing that if he couldn't control his emotions, no rational conversation would be taking place.

Attempting to pull her arm out of his firm grasp, and failing, she felt her anger intensify. "No, what I need is to get the hell away from you, Chase." This wasn't her world, and he wasn't the man she wished he could be. She fought back tears and tugged on her arm again, wanting to put as much space between them as humanly possible.

He wasn't relenting. She was not in any type of emotional state to drive home safely. If she didn't want to discuss what had happened like a rational adult, he was at least driving her home. Pulling her away from the door, he closed it and took the keys she was holding in her other hand. "If you don't want to talk, then get in my car. I'm taking you home."

"Screw you, Chase. Give me my damn keys and let me leave." She was beyond rational thinking at the moment, and just wanted to get away from him so she could think. Tears trickled down her cheeks and she angrily swiped them away with the back of her hand.

What the hell was going on here? There was no doubt in his mind that she was not thinking clearly and he sure as hell wasn't giving her keys to a car at the moment. "If you'll stop acting like a child for a moment and calm down, I'll get you home safely."

"You are such a domineering prick," she all but screamed, wanting her keys back and wishing she had the nerve to slap his face for being so unfeeling.

Floored at the anger in his words, he released her arm. "Obviously I'm missing something here, because I thought we enjoyed each other tonight." Wasn't that what she'd wanted? He was confused.

Rolling her eyes, she stalked over to his car, shaking her head. How could any man be so dense? "Just take me home since you've obviously confiscated my car for the night." She didn't want to talk to him. She wanted to lock herself in her safe little world and forget he ever existed.

He didn't argue with her as she slid into the passenger seat of his car. Turning over the ignition, he gripped the steering wheel tightly, forcing himself not to demand she give him some explanation for her strange behavior. She stared out the window for the entire ride back to her apartment, and he wanted to take her over his knee for being so damn stubborn. Before he pulled up in front of her complex, he made one last comment. "When you've calmed down Jessie, we should talk about why you're so angry."

Keeping her head turned from him, she waited until he stopped the car to respond, then said, "Go to hell, Chase." Sliding out of the vehicle, she all but ran to her apartment. Then she realized she didn't even have her keys to let herself in.

Taking a frustrated breath, he walked to her door, and held out the keys to her. She snatched them from his hands without once glancing his way. As the door slammed in his face, he turned back around and decided that whatever the hell was going through that mind of hers would have to wait until she was willing to be reasonable   again.

CHAPTER FOURTEEN

Woman's Thoughts

He made it to work with his mind still on last night. But he forced himself to push thoughts of Jessie to the back of his mind for the morning. There were a million things to do. The club had been a vacation compared to running his father's business. At lunch, he left a message for Jessie to call him so they could talk, but he had little time to check his service in the afternoon, as dozens of employees bombarded his office, worried about their employment status now that his father was no longer in charge.

By six that evening he was ready for some down time, and his head was pounding with thoughts of issues raised at the staff meeting. He'd been away from this for a few years, so catching up and proving his leadership skills was going to be a challenge. When he finally had a minute to himself, he listened to his voice mail, and was disappointed she hadn't returned his call.

He knew letting her cool down before he attempted contact again was the smart thing to do. Carolyn had invited him for drinks tonight, and he considered cancelling since his stress level was so high, but then decided he couldn't do that after everything she'd done for him lately.

After grabbing his suit jacket from his chair, he made his way over to her house, hoping she'd understand when he begged off early to get some much needed rest. He certainly hadn't slept last night after the insanity with Jessie. Even his dreams had been filled with the raven-haired beauty.

"You look like hell, Chase," Carolyn said, letting him in.

"Corporate life." He forced a grin as he walked with her to the den, familiar enough with her home to know his own way.

After pouring him a scotch and water on the rocks, she walked over, handed it to him, before moving back to the bar to fix a martini. "Want to talk about it?"

She joined him on the couch, and he tried to decide if he wanted to bring up the subject. They'd always been upfront with each other, and the only reason he was concerned now was because he wasn't sure what to say. For a man who prided himself on self-discipline, he was floundering lately.

He took a healthy drink of his scotch, and she raised a questioning brow. "I know it's still new, Chase, but your father's passing will get easier."

"Dad lived a good life before that illness found him, Carolyn, and I'm coming to peace with that. It's Jessie I just don't understand." He shouldn't be burdening her with his problems, but she was one of the few people in his life he could talk to.

"What happened? I know you were trying to get in touch with her."

"Honestly, I have no idea what's going on in that woman's mind. We had some great nights together and then she disappeared for a week, and when she came back, I'd already accepted that she was just looking for a little sexual adventure. I gave her a great night in the dungeon and after our fun, well; she acted like I'd taken advantage of her." He still didn't understand why she was so angry, and since she hadn't returned his call, he wasn't sure he ever would.

Sitting back on the couch, her mouth fell open. "Let me get this straight, you think Jessie just wanted casual sex?"

"That's the impression I got, yes." Shrugging his shoulders, he took a deep sip of his scotch.

Shaking her head, she laughed disbelievingly. "That doesn't really fit the impression Amanda gave me about Jessie. To be honest I thought she was still a virgin. Something isn't adding up."

Taking another sip of his scotch, he explained their few nights together, knowing Carolyn wasn't the type of person to repeat what they discussed here. He didn't leave out details. They'd discussed their relationships in the past; there were few secrets between them.

"So let me get this straight. This woman was a virgin and had all this emotional crap in her past because of a boyfriend who finally admitted his true nature, and you thought it was all about sex for her?" Shaking her head she gave him a look that spoke volumes.

When she put it that way, it didn't make sense to him either, and he wondered if he'd completely misjudged the feelings Jessie had for him. "You don't think this was about sex at all, do you?" He really didn't need for her to admit he'd been a dumb-ass. When he thought about the night more carefully, he realized only a blind fool would have not understood what had happened.

"I love you as a friend and admire you as a dominant, but Chase, at the moment you need your ass kicked for not being more observant." Lifting her lip in a sneer, she chided him. "It doesn't take a genius to figure out a woman doesn't wait all that time to give it up to a man she doesn't at least feel something for."

He didn't know much about how women felt about their first experiences. Virgins weren't exactly commonplace in his world of sexual pleasures, but what Carolyn was saying made perfect sense. "So you're telling me I've been a complete ass and should crawl over to her place on my hands and knees and beg her forgiveness?" That thought may have bothered him if it had been anyone other than Jessie.

"It's not my place to tell you what you should do, but if nothing else, you should apologize for not taking the time to understand her better. That's really not like you, Chase. I've seen how compassionate you are with submissive's. Hell, my slaves would love to have me so concerned with their needs." She chuckled

"I'll be honest, Carolyn, I haven't thought clearly since the night I first met her. You know me. I care for the people I play with, but I've never felt anything with anyone like this before. With Jessie, I find myself unable to concentrate at all."

"It sounds to me like you've fallen in love." Laughing softly, she sipped on her martini and watched his expression.

The moment she said the word love, everything seemed to fall in place. He was acting like a man in love, he thought, and it shocked him to his very core. Jealous, possessive, wanting to stake his claim--any

creature in nature reacted the same way when it took a
mate. Throwing his head back, he chuckled deeply.

Carolyn joined in his laughter. "You know this is
what makes females the superior race right? The ability to understand emotions. You men may never get
that one." She elbowed him, looking superior.

"Understanding emotions and being able to restrain
them when needed are two separate things," he joked
back, knowing that statement always got her ire up.
"This makes the male more superior because we can
temper our emotions when dealing with situations that
require a clear head." He smirked, but was more than
impressed at how easily she understood what he was
feeling when he himself hadn't been able to come to a
resolution.

Rolling her eyes, she guffawed. "Keep telling yourself that, Chase, especially while you're eating crow
apologizing to Jessie." Smirking in superiority.

Joking aside, he wasn't sure Jessie would forgive
him for the stupidity he'd shown in not understanding
her feelings. That thought sobered him immediately.
"How am I going to make this up to her?"

"From what you've told me, she's already got a
wealth of issues outside of this, Chase. All I can suggest
is you tell her how you truly feel and see how she re-
sponds."

Jessie had needed someone to show her there was
more to a relationship than heartbreak, and he'd failed

miserably. He wasn't even sure if he deserved her forgiveness, but that didn't mean he was willing to give up without trying. "Well, if nothing else, I can at least let her know it was way more to me than just a booty call." How he'd been so blind was beyond him.

"That's definitely a start," Carolyn agreed.

They enjoyed the rest of their evening, catching up on what was going on at the club, and Chase explained his trials with managing the new company. It was nice to have a female as a friend who expected nothing but friendship. Before he'd met Carolyn, he hadn't even thought such a relationship was possible. When he made it home that evening, he fell asleep thinking of ways that he could make up for what a complete ass he'd been to Jessie.

CHAPTER FIFTEEN

Baby Steps

Ignoring the calls from Chase over the next few days was much easier said than done. She'd listened to his sexy voice asking for a chance to apologize several times, and had almost given in. But knowing where any conversation with him would lead, she refused to let herself fall into that trap. Seeing Greg, on the other hand, who'd called out of the blue and invited her to lunch, was something she felt she couldn't avoid.

She hadn't heard from him in so long, and it was amazing that the sense of pain she used to feel when they talked was no longer there. She dressed in a pair of worn jeans and a comfortable t-shirt since they were just going to an outdoor cafe, but she did take the time to fix her hair and makeup, wanting to look her best.

He still looked as handsome as ever, she thought as she walked up on the sidewalk. Smiling warmly, she said, "It's good to see you again, Greg." She meant it. He'd been her friend more than her boyfriend.

"You look incredible, Jessie." He pulled her into a hug.

Hugging him back, she felt at this point in her life, she could finally be happy for him. "I missed you, Greg," she said. It was the truth. She had missed the friend he had once been, and it was sad they hadn't kept in touch. But it had taken a while to deal with her pain.

"I missed you too, Jess," he said, laughing. He finally let her go and stood back looking into her eyes. "Obviously, life has been treating you well."

She wasn't about to talk to him about her issues with Chase, so she nodded, trying not to spoil the mood. "You look like you've been basking in the sun." She couldn't deny he was a sexy man, even if he did play for the other team.

"Barry and I just got back from a cruise to Jamaica."

"I am so jealous!" She punched him playfully in the arm, and they found a table. They used to talk about taking a cruise, but it had never panned out. "So tell me all about the trip. Was it as beautiful as it looked in the brochures we use to get?" It felt incredible to have a normal conversation with him, and she was smiling from ear to ear.

"The Falls were incredible, Jess. You would have loved them, but the poverty in the city was just heart-breaking, so it had its pros and cons." When the server appeared, they both ordered lunch before he went into detail about the ship itself and the sumo karaoke.

"It sounds like you guys had a ball. I'm going to have to do a cruise one day." The rest of their lunch they filled each other in on what was going on in their lives. Jess left out Chase, but told him about her recent Florida trip and telecommuting job.

Greg paid their bill and walked her back to her car. "Listen, Jess, I hope we can do this again. I know I laid a lot of burdens at your feet with what I was going through, and I want you to know how sorry I am about that."

"None of us can change who we are Greg." She smiled at him, feeling no remorse for what they'd shared for the first time in years. "I miss hanging out with you, and I hope you won't be a stranger now." It was so freeing to finally let go of some of the emotional baggage that had been weighing her down.

"No, we can't change, Jess, and believe me, if I were straight, there could never be another woman I'd love to give my heart to more. I hope you know that." Pulling her into his arms again, he hugged her tightly, smiling.

"If you were straight, I would never let you out of my sight." She hugged him back. His comments meant more to her than she could ever express.

They exchanged phone numbers again before parting ways and promised to meet up again soon. Heading back to her apartment, she felt lightness in her step that filled her heart with hope. Tackling work for the next few hours kept her occupied until it was time to get dressed for the book club meeting. She'd missed last week because of her trip and was interested in discussing the book she'd read while lounging at the beach.

She dressed in a strapless sundress, the hint of color from her trip accentuating the white garment, and she left off pantyhose, since her legs had a tan, for a change. Tonight she was determined to get to know even more about the women she met with weekly. It was time for her to stop shutting out people in her life and make more friends.

Amanda came over and hugged her as she walked into Dana's house and she returned the gesture. "We haven't done our weekly lunch yet and I've got tons to tell you." She wanted to share her experience with Greg, and just catch up.

"Carolyn's invited me over tomorrow. If you don't mind doing it at her place, I'm sure she would be fine with you joining us." Amanda pulled her into the room as she talked.

Jessie thought about scheduling another day for lunch, but decided that was the old Jessie. "If you don't mind asking Carolyn tonight, that sounds like a great idea."

Amanda told her she would ask her after the meeting, and they took their seats as refreshments were handed out. When the conversations started, instead of hanging her head, Jessie contributed her thoughts, and when it came to the topic of BDSM, she decided she needed to speak her mind.

"I think some people construe this lifestyle in the wrong way." Jessie lifted her chin and glanced at Amanda then the ladies gathered. "A person that calls himself a dominant but just gets his kicks hurting women is an asshole, not a master." She worried about bringing this up, knowing what Amanda had suffered, but she felt it needed to be addressed.

"We're all friends here so it's no secret I was attacked. I admit at first I blamed the lifestyle for that prick, but the truth is you're right Jess. There are abusive men out there; you hear stories that have nothing to do with BDSM. I just think no matter who your date, you need to be cautious."

"My mother's second husband was an alcoholic," Lauren confessed. "I have to second what Amanda's saying," shaking her head she continued. "A man either respects a woman or he doesn't. He could be a preacher, a doctor, or a dominant; it's the mindset that truly matters."

"That may be true, but respect in my world doesn't involve spanking me like a naughty child." Tamara curled her lip. "I assume people into sadomasochism were abused as children."

"That's because all the romances on this topic we've read have been about some man who has a screwed up past. We don't ever get the viewpoint of the average person finding this just because it interests them. There are people who enjoy this just because it turns them on." That seemed like the case with Chase. He enjoyed being in control and as far as she knew, his childhood hadn't been that horrific.

"I don't know about the men, but how can any woman be willing to offer herself up in that context without going against everything we've fought for?" Tamela sneered at the thought of some man controlling her.

"Tamela, haven't you ever wondered what it would be like to not have to make all the decisions for a change, and just allow a man to pleasure you in ways he'd know would bring you over the edge?" Jessie was really curious about her answer because she knew what a powerful woman Tamela was in the business world, and she wondered if anyone ever saw the emotional side of her.

"I have yet to meet a man I would trust in that capacity, but not having to make all the rules in the bedroom might be a nice change of pace." She laughed and the rest of the women joined in.

"I don't think anyone would deny this isn't something you would try with a stranger." Carolyn said. "With the right partner, this can be a beautiful way of expressing your sexuality, but again, you have to really trust the person you're playing with."

Excusing herself, Jessie walked to the bathroom and fought her own emotions. She hadn't thought this was something she wanted to pursue with anyone but Chase, but just talking about it tonight made her long to experience more. The truth was she loved that she didn't have to decide what brought her pleasure and could just enjoy the sensations. Maybe she could find that with another man. Jessie also knew she couldn't allow herself to get involved in a relationship where the lines weren't clearly drawn. With Chase, she would always want more than just passion, but maybe this was something she should at least think about exploring with someone else.

After getting her emotions under control, she rejoined the group. They discussed several other aspects of the BDSM relationship, but her own thoughts crowded her mind as she tried to decide what she really needed to make her happy. She decided to talk with Carolyn about this after everyone else had left.

She waited until the other ladies had left before walking over to Carolyn. The woman had been so great to Amanda when she was dealing with the crazy man, as she and Amanda both called him; maybe they'd just gotten off on the wrong foot. "Do you have a few minutes?"

"Absolutely," Carolyn said. With a smile, she led her over to the bar. "What's on your mind?"

Accepting the wine Carolyn poured, Jessie tried to decide how to voice her thoughts. "I think I under-stand what you were trying to warn me about with Chase now." It had taken seeing both sides of his per-sonality to truly get the man he really was.

"I probably spoke out of turn."

"Actually, I think you were right. I think I allowed my own perception of what I needed in a relationship to blind me to the person he truly is."

Shaking her head, Carolyn stared at her. "Maybe you'd better explain?" Sitting down on the couch, she patted it, inviting Jessie to join her.

"All his baggage dealing with his father's illness left him vulnerable and he needed someone to distract him." She was speaking more to herself than Carolyn at the moment.

"Is that what you think?" Sitting back on the couch, Carolyn raised a brow.

Nodding her head, she took a sip of liquid courage. "The man he showed me in the dungeon was nothing like the person I fell in love with."

Gasping, Carolyn's eyes widened. "So what were the differences in him?"

Jessie knew she probably shouldn't be discussing Chase with his friend, but if anyone knew him, Carolyn did. "He was almost cold and disconnected in his master role. That was the biggest one, I guess." Not the entire time, she remembered. He'd been pretty hot when he loved her body.

"So you think he only made love to you because he was feeling sorry for himself?"

"Why else would he do a complete 360?" She could only assume the person he'd been in the dungeon was the real man, not the tender lover that made her feel cherished.

Laughing softly, she tapped her finger to her lips for a few seconds. "Have you talked with him about your feelings?"

"And have Chase pity me for falling in love with him?" Making a face, her frown deepened. "I don't need his sympathy."

"The things I could teach you," Carolyn said, laughing softly, and then sighing. "Did you stop to consider that maybe he felt something more for you?"

Shooting her a look that said, *yeah right* she spoke. "The man is drop-dead gorgeous. Why would he feel anything more for me?"

"You really don't have a high opinion of yourself, do you?"

Jessie frowned again. "I guess I don't."

"You're a beautiful woman, and if I had any indication that you liked other women, and I didn't know that Chase would skin me alive, I'd offer to help you overcome that."

Stunned at her words, Jessie's eyes widened enormously. "I guess I should be flattered?"

Laughing, Carolyn said, "Don't worry, you're safe with me. But seriously, have you considered that being in a relationship with a master might really help you overcome those feelings of self-doubt?"

"I think the whole sex with stranger's thing pretty much takes any chance of me going that route away."

"I rarely have sex with my slaves. People just assume that's what happens." Sipping on her wine, Carolyn smiled warmly.

"How can it not be sexual?" That thought hadn't even registered as a possibility.

"I didn't say it wasn't sexual, only that I didn't normally have sex with my slaves. There's a difference. They derive pleasure from the things I do to them, and vice versa, but intercourse isn't mandatory."

"There are other people who keep sex completely on the outside?" That might be something she was willing to consider.

"More than you would imagine."

"That's interesting." It was more than interesting, Jessie thought. She couldn't deny she was interested in hearing more.

"I know someone who might consider mentoring you."

"I don't know. I really want to learn more, but I'm not sure I'm really ready for any of this." She had enjoyed exploring with Chase, even if she couldn't keep her heart out of it, but a stranger...

"Of course it's your choice. I just don't want you to think every relationship in my world has to be so complicated."

"I guess it wouldn't hurt to at least talk with another dominant." Saying that was a huge leap for her. A few weeks ago she would have turned her lip up and considered people into this strange. She glanced at her watch and realized they'd been talking for over an hour. "I guess I need to be getting home."

"I'll walk you out." Looking at her distracted, she led to the front door. "I'll talk to my friend and let you know when he can set up something."

Jessie nodded her agreement as she walked back to her car. Talking with Carolyn had been a good idea and she felt better. Even if she still wasn't over Chase, she wasn't feeling as overwhelmed as before.

CHAPTER SIXTEEN

Deception

Hanging up the phone, he sat down and stared at it. Chase was shocked by Carolyn's conversation. He considered himself a man who played by the rules, and what he was considering couldn't be labeled honest. Knowing Jessie was willing to speak with another dominant, even if in a mentorship capacity, had angered him since she wouldn't even return his calls. Jealously wasn't an emotion he normally experienced, but in this instance, it forced his hand.

For hours he'd debated over the plan going through his mind. He debated the possible outcomes until his head was pounding. Finally he concluded that this was the only option that he could live with. It would only be a small deception, he decided.

The charade would be brief. Chase only intended to spend a few minutes talking to her alone, but over the next several hours, his mind considered taking things to a level that would demand she at least be honest about her feelings toward him. He only hoped his little plan didn't backfire and make Jessie mistrust him more than she already did.

When he called Carolyn back to explain what he wanted, she attempted to dissuade him. She was adamant about not betraying Jessie's trust. Carolyn also made it very clear she was not pleased she'd decided to confide in him. None of her arguments deterred him from the path he'd chosen to take.

He convinced her after a long argument that he only had Jessie's best interests at heart. Hoping it wasn't just a selfish need on his part to be the only man in her life, he thought about how he would play this tonight to make sure she wasn't hurt. All he wanted was an opportunity. A chance to show her he was capable of bringing her body to incredible heights, but also to tell her his heart was just as involved.

Tonight he would at least know if there was any chance. If there wasn't, he would let her walk out of his life knowing he cared deeply.

He called Carolyn again and gave her explicit instructions on how to set up the personal room at the club. He wanted to bring her back to his own dungeon, but until this was settled, the club would suffice. *She wasn't walking out of the club tonight until she understands how much I care.*

If he had to tie her down to make her listen, he was going to make his feelings clear. The rational side told him he couldn't keep her in the dungeon against her will. *Why don't you club her over the head and drag her to your cave,* his conscious mocked. *I just want to show I love her,* he argued back mentally.

The plans he made were going to be very difficult to pull off without talking, and Jessie would assume that was all that was going to happen tonight. He wracked his brain for a solution, knowing even as he planned if she forgave him, he was going to be kissing her feet for a long time. Carolyn was going to be sick of hearing his voice, he thought as he called her yet again.

He knew he had her at a disadvantage because she couldn't argue any of his ideas with Jessie in the room. She'd agreed to all his demands and told him she and Jessie would be waiting for him tonight at eight. Hanging up with her, he attempted to focus on work again.

During his lunch break, he went to the club, and left a detailed list for Carolyn in the private office. He knew he was being overly cautious, but tonight had to be planned out perfectly. He felt like a dick for the game he was about to play, but he fought off the feeling, convincing himself the end result would be worth it for both of them.

He managed to drag himself back to the office, his mind anywhere but on the job. A board meeting later and he felt ready to curse in frustration at being stuck here when he had a beautiful woman to convince to give him another chance. As soon as it was professionally possible, he left the dull business world behind and went home to prepare for the meeting he wanted to attend tonight.

CHAPTER SEVENTEEN

Games

Carolyn hung up with Chase, and joined Amanda and Jessie again for lunch. *He wouldn't give someone an impossible task,* she thought to herself as she tried to pay attention to the conversation at the table. When Amanda excused herself to return to work, she knew it was time to play her part in this deception. She only hoped Jessie would forgive her later.

"Now that she's gone, I wanted to let you know I've set you up with the friend we discussed." She saw Jessie's eyes widen, and smiled comfortingly. "Trust me, Jessie, I wouldn't hesitate to entrust anyone to this man."

"Maybe this was just a bad idea, Carolyn. This is all just happening a little too fast." Nibbling her lip, she frowned.

"Of course it's your decision Jessie, but you'll never really know if this is something you want unless you give it a chance." If it had been anyone other than Chase, she would have simply backed off. But she knew both Jessie and Chase needed tonight.

"Did you talk to him about the no sex clause?" Flushing, she looked at her hands.

"He was completely agreeable with your terms, and also stated he didn't have sex with a submissive unless she agreed to be his long term." That was the truth, Carolyn told the little voice chiding her for being part of this ruse, no matter what was at stake.

"And you'll vouch for this guy? I mean, he's not some pervert who just gets his kicks from hurting women, right?" Jessie shivered at the thought.

"Well, we all consider ourselves pervs." She chuckled. "But I would stand by this person with my own life, if need be. That's how much I trust him." Again, she was telling the truth, which made this a little more palatable for her.

Taking a deep breath, she nodded. "I guess I'm meeting your friend tonight."

She could see the worry in her eyes and smiled. "You won't regret this, Jessie. He's an incredible dominant and I think if anyone would be a perfect fit for you, he is." If Chase screwed this up, she would personally kick his ass. "There are a few conditions."

"That doesn't sound like something I'm going to like. What are they?"

"Well, he expects a submissive to be blindfolded and tethered when he enters the room. He will run you through his paces and if at any time you decide you want to stop, that's the end of it."

"I thought I was just going to talk to the man?" Jessie's voice rose in panic.

"He just wants to make sure anyone he mentors truly wants to explore her submissive side. Trust me, this isn't that unusual." *You're going straight to hell*, Carolyn's conscience screamed at her.

"So I can't even see the person? How am I supposed to know what he's going to do with me? This really doesn't sound safe. It doesn't even sound logical."

"Like I told you before, I know this man well, but if you'd feel better, I could stay in the room with you." She had no intention of doing that, either, because Chase would never hurt Jessie, but something told her that Jessie was on the edge of refusing to go through with this.

"I guess you being in the room would make it safe. How does this guy, um, play, I guess would be the word?"

"He's really into the sensual side of BDSM, Jessie, so don't worry about the pain thing. It's not his style. That's why I think the two of you will probably enjoy each other."

"I guess as long as you don't leave us alone, that's acceptable."

They said their goodbyes and Jessie drove home to finish her work before the event later tonight. Nervous didn't even begin to explain how she felt about what she was going to do. Every logical part of her mind screamed at her to call off this insanity. Meeting some strange man to explore her sensuality was so far out of character, she began to wonder if she didn't need counseling.

She couldn't focus on work, and decided she'd have to concentrate on it after this thing tonight. Her mind was all over the place, wondering what it would feel like to experience this with someone she didn't really know. What would he expect from her? Knowing Carolyn wouldn't leave her was the only comforting aspect of this entire situation.

She wasn't sure how she felt about Carolyn witnessing what was going to happen though. Oddly enough, the thought didn't disgust her. Maybe she was a just a closet deviant, she thought. Deciding a long bath would calm her nerves, she soaked for almost an hour. She wanted to call Amanda, but knew this was one topic they couldn't discuss. Even after Amanda's words at the book club meeting, she wasn't sure she didn't harbor bad feelings against the leather community.

Stepping out of the bath, she laughed at how intelligent she sounded about the subject. After drying off she found Sebastian and they had a nice long talk together. Her laptop, she discovered had tons of research on the topic of alternative lifestyles. With her feline companion by her side, she read and spoke to Sebastian like he was human. Most of what she saw online made her sneer, but there were some aspects that resonated in her *I might be willing to explore this* thoughts.

Jessie's nerves were strung so tight that when she put her laptop away, she considered calling tonight off. Sebastian watched her in apparent boredom as she dressed meticulously. "I know what you're thinking," she glanced at Sebastian with accusation, "but you can't be the only man in my life." Reaching down to stroke the spot behind his ears, she smiled. Sebastian didn't seem convinced. Before she left for the club she placed a can of tuna in his food dish in the kitchen.

Pulling up to the club she continued to second guess her decision. Sipping on a glass of wine, enjoying a great book, that's what she was missing out on by being here. Taking a deep breath, she forced her feet to walk inside Sensation's.

CHAPTER EIGHTEEN

Dungeon

Chase nervously paced the office at the club as he waited on Jessie to arrive. Knowing her, he wasn't even sure she'd show up. He'd already decided if she didn't come, he was headed straight to her apartment to at least explain how he felt. Leaving things unsettled was something he never did, and he certainly couldn't do that with his Jessie girl. Communication was the most important part of any relationship, so even if this did work out tonight, he would still have to bring that up and drive the point home.

He couldn't deny Carolyn had been right about his lack of understanding concerning the female mind. As a dominant, he prided himself on being able to read a submissive's face during a scene, but he obviously had a long way to go before understanding a woman's heart. He'd decided to start reading some of those romance novels women seemed to enjoy, and had been amazed at the space allotted to the characters' feelings.

He'd also been appalled at how, in one particularly popular novel, the master had treated the innocent submissive. It made him wonder why there were so many people interested in this lifestyle now. The degradation depicted should have made them not want anything to do with BDSM.

His thoughts were interrupted as Carolyn entered the room, letting him know Jessie was preparing for their meeting. His heart lurched at the thought of what he was about to do tonight with her. The last thing he wanted was to give her an experience that would turn her away from this permanently.

He always planned out everything he did in a scene carefully. Chase enjoyed having the ability to be in control, but in the end, it was all about what made the submissive enjoy the experience. This time that person was Jessie, so what had always mattered in the past was even more important because if he disappointed her, he destroyed himself in the process.

Carolyn had taken the form-fitting biker shorts and sports bra he'd picked out for her tonight back to the room. He'd chosen the outfit because he knew she'd never agree to be nude with a stranger. The material would allow him to access all her pleasure points and not have her feel completely vulnerable.

Waiting outside the room for Carolyn to let him know she was ready, he took a deep breath to calm his nerves. He'd never known performance anxiety before, but his confidence was shaky, considering what rested on the outcome of tonight. When she opened the door, the sight of Jessie tethered to the cross almost took his breath away.

"Jessie, your master is here, and I want to remind you that during this scene he's asked you not to speak unless you are ready to stop the scene." Carolyn gave Chase a wink for good luck and left the room.

Jessie clenched her hands into fists. They were raised over her head and attached to the cross by cuffs. Taking several deep breaths, she almost opened her mouth to stop this before it started. She was so nervous, her heart was racing in her chest and her mouth felt so dry, she could barely swallow. At the touch of a strong finger tracing gently down her cheek, she caught her breath.

Her body was so stiff, he wanted to encourage her to relax, but giving away his identity would destroy his entire plan. Instead, he focused on allowing his large hands to trail from her wrists to her shoulders, attempting to soothe her with the innocent caress. From her shoulders, his hand moved with unhurried movements to her throat and up to her jaw. Lifting her chin, he allowed his head to lower and moved his face to the exposed flesh of her neck, inhaling her soft floral scent. His other hand moved quickly across her breast and rested on her abdomen, making a soothing circular motion.

His tenderness was comforting, and without thought, she arched her neck back to rest on the hard chest behind her. Feeling his lips splay small kisses against the tender flesh of her neck, then move upward to lightly nip her earlobe, she trembled. His mouth did things to her body she'd never expected from a stranger. His actions sent tiny sparks of pleasure through her limbs, and she sighed softly.

Pleased that she was enjoying his touch, he allowed a hand to cup her bra-covered breast. Her gasp of shock as his thumb and forefinger rolled the coral peak before pinching lightly was sweet music to his ears. It let him know she was responding to him, and it was something he'd worried she wouldn't be able to do under the circumstances.

A stranger's hands shouldn't feel this good; her mind told her even as her body accepted the pleasure. Closing her eyes behind the blindfold, she refused to listen to her mind and just felt. His hands were magical, she thought as one traveled across her abdomen again, and cupped her sex.

He wanted to slide his hand beneath the waistband of the form-fitting shorts and caress the silken smoothness of her sex, but he knew that would be too much for her. Instead, he allowed his finger to run slowly over her, massaging gently until soft gasps of pleasure fell from her lips. The dampness through the material was evidence she was enjoying his touch. He continued until he felt her begin to tense. Pulling his hands away, he backed up to retrieve a thick, butter-soft leather flogger.

The loss of his hands on her flesh made her ache when she'd been so close to finding release from his touch. All thoughts of not being able to enjoy something like this with a stranger were erased from her mind. Her body craved this, and wrong or right, she wanted more. Twisting her wrists in the restrictive cuffs, she whimpered.

The image of her beautiful body writhing against the cross would remain in his memories for as long as he lived. Walking back to her, he arranged her silken hair over her shoulder before lightly allowing the flogger to swoosh against her back. He wanted her to find pleasure in the ministrations, and slowly built up his tempo as the dance began. It was amazing how her body moved for him as he increased the pressure with each stroke.

She had no idea that this could be so enjoyable. The increasing intensity of the flogger had her gasping, but not in pain. There was just an incredible sensation of being slightly pushed forward and then her body recovering. She gave herself over completely to the experience.

The soft sounds escaping her beautiful lips encouraged him to continue. A soft sheen of sweat covered his brow as he masterfully conquered her body. Only when Jessie began to slump against the cuffs that held her up did he finally stop the dance.

In that brief, still moment, a feeling of pleasure overwhelmed her. She cried out. Then nothingness overcame her, followed by peaceful lethargy. It was singularly the most beautiful experience she'd ever had.

Unclasping the cuffs that bound her, he lifted her easily into his arms and placed her face up on the large, leather covered table. He caressed the strands of hair away from her face and rubbed her arms softly until she was focused once more. She had found sub-space so easily and again, he was amazed by the beauty of the woman surrendering to him.

Capturing her wrists carefully, he attached them to the large clamps on the table. His large hand encircled her ankle, and he expertly clasped it to the table, then spread her beautiful thighs wide and bound the other ankle with the same ease.

Allowing his eyes to roam over her, he wished she could see how sensual she looked, even partially clothed, splayed out this way. It was another vision he knew he'd remember always. The subspace had probably altered her perception of what she could handle, so he decided to not attempt anything overwhelming. Instead, he once again focused on bringing her body pleasure.

His mouth closed over her breast through the fabric and she arched off the table to push against him. Biting down gently on the stiff coral peak, he was awarded with a soft cry of pleasure. His hand moved down between her parted thighs and stroked her heated flesh, finding great pleasure in how wet she was already. The flogger was obviously a toy she enjoyed and it pleased him to know that his world was now becoming hers.

Her mind and body were flooded with sensations. His touch was only enflaming her more. She wished she could continue to experience the bliss. Jessie couldn't believe it was possible to feel this way. It shocked her that it no longer mattered who the stranger was giving her the feelings, only that they continued. It felt like she was on a drug-induced high that she never wanted to come down from.

Sliding his fingers under the band of her shorts, he slowly worked them across her bare flesh. He had so many more things to share with her tonight, but at the moment he just wanted to watch her come undone. He allowed a lone digit to push into her tight sheath, and almost groaned at the tightness of the velvety chamber as it resisted his entry.

Tensing at the feel of his finger inside her, she slowly came back to her senses. The pleasure was incredible, and she wanted it to continue, but this wasn't right. Tightening her pelvic muscles she pushed against the invasion. "Stop," she whispered, caught between the incredible sensations and knowing she didn't know this man well enough to allow it to continue.

He felt her flesh grip his finger as he slowly withdrew, and knew he had to give in to her command. Without doubt, he could have continued to stroke her and possibly encouraged her to give in, but that went against everything he believed about his lifestyle. "Are you sure that's what you want?" He spoke the words softly, giving her one last chance to change her mind.

The voice was hauntingly familiar, although through the haze of what she'd just experienced, she was having trouble placing it. Nodding her head slightly, she knew this had to end, even if her body ached for fulfillment.

Moving to the head of the table, he lifted her head and removed the blindfold. He had no idea what her reaction would be when she discovered it had been him giving her pleasure. He kept her tethered to the table, wanting to at least have a chance to talk with her if she was angry.

"Chase?" A small part of her was pleased a stranger hadn't unleashed such passion, but the other part was infuriated that he had deceived her this way. "Why?" She couldn't seem to form more than one word responses at the moment.

"I couldn't stand the thought of another man pleasing you this way, Jessie." He couldn't be anything other than honest with her. Seeing the pain in her eyes made him feel like the ass he was at the moment.

They had both played her. That was the first thought that crossed her mind at his answer. How could she trust Carolyn, but more importantly him, ever again? "Untie me," she demanded softly, not sure if she could control her anger much longer, or the tears that threatened to fall at being played so well.

"I'll do that, Jessie, but first I want you to hear me out." He could see the fire that filled her eyes and decided if he wanted to offer an explanation, he'd better begin now. "I love you, Jessie." The words escaped his lips before any other thought could form in his mind.

Her eyes widened as he spoke the words she had longed to hear. Everything in her wanted to say the words back to him, but something held her back. "No, Chase, you don't." It wasn't possible that this beautiful man loved her. It was probably just his way of making up for this deceitful trick. Her heart was aching, wishing that it was possible, and knowing without doubt he just couldn't feel that way about her. "Let me up, Chase." She was two seconds away from losing it, and being chained to this table wasn't how she wanted it to happen.

He could see in her eyes she didn't believe him, but he had no idea how to prove he was telling her the truth. "Jessie, I'm going to untie you, but for the love of God, don't go storming off again before we have the chance to talk." He didn't wait for her agreement, since holding her against her will was not something he wanted. He quickly released the binds.

Standing up, she walked over to where her clothes were neatly folded, and slid them over the outfit she was wearing. She needed a few minutes to collect her thoughts because at the moment she wanted to slap his face for lying to her about his feelings. Whatever game he was playing with her, she didn't appreciate it at all, and as soon as she collected herself, she planned on letting him know just that.

He watched her dress, and felt his heart ache, knowing how deceived she felt. Tonight was not supposed to end this way. He'd hoped to show her how much pleasure he could offer her, confess his feelings and assure her they could live happily ever after. Obviously, she wasn't on board with anything he was thinking at the moment.

When she felt she could speak without screaming at him, she turned to face him. "Okay, you want to talk, let's find some place other than here to do it. I honestly don't want to be in this room one moment longer."

"Would my office here suffice?" Technically it was Carolyn's office at the moment, but he was sure she wouldn't mind. He was just pleased Jessie wasn't running away from him.

"No, it will not. I want to leave this building. I'd prefer not to be anywhere close to this place." Every second she stood here, she grew angrier. She had thought Carolyn was becoming her friend, but obviously that wasn't the case or she wouldn't have betrayed her trust in such a way. And him--well, she wouldn't even be able to put into words how pissed off she was without screaming.

"Where would you like to go, Jessie?" Considering the way she was looking at him right now, he knew where she'd like to send him, and he wasn't sure he didn't deserve it.

"The overlook," she decided on a whim. That was where this started; what better place for an ending? The thought hurt her heart more than she was willing to admit. "Follow me in your car." With those words, she stormed out of the room and the building. Carolyn, she would talk with later, and hopefully she'd be in a much better frame of mind than she was at the moment.

As she slid behind the wheel of her car, she decided she really didn't care if he followed her or not. It had taken all her bravery to explore the new feelings she had and she felt cheated by the hand she'd been dealt tonight. Maybe she was being unreasonable, she thought as she drove, but she wasn't a person who trusted easily, so having her trust betrayed wasn't an easily forgivable offense.

When they reached their destination, Chase knew by the look in her eyes he was in for a dressing down. It had seemed like a great plan. Show her how much he could give and confess his feelings. Obviously, he hadn't taken into consideration how betrayed Jessie would feel when his cover had been blown. At least she was willing to talk to him. That left him a little hope.

Meanwhile, the fifteen minute drive had given her enough time to consider the situation more rationally. She'd gone over every aspect of the evening, labeling each a pro or con. On the pro side, she hadn't just let some strange man bring her to bliss. On the con side, Chase had blatantly deceived her. She wasn't at all sure what to do with that information.

He slid out of his car and walked over to her as she exited. "Before we start talking, Jessie, I want you to know I wasn't lying about how I feel about you." If nothing else came out of their conversation, he wanted that point made. She could be pissed off at him--hell, she could scream and rant if she wanted; it wasn't like he didn't deserve it--but he also wanted her to believe his feelings were real.

The argument she had ready to escape her lips was all but deflated the minute he spoke those words. Still, she couldn't believe a man like him could really love her, and had to admonish him. "Chase, you shouldn't tell a person that just to get away with being a complete ass." She had no idea what his real motive had been tonight. Then again, he was an alpha man who, no doubt, didn't take well to letting other men touch something he thought was his.

"So I'm an ass because I love you?" He wanted her to laugh. Hell, he would give his right arm if she'd crack a smile.

That so wasn't what she meant and he had to know it. "No, you're an ass because you're telling me what I want to hear so I won't make you feel bad for deceiving me." He was a charmer, she'd give him that, and she wanted to believe him so badly. It hurt to think he'd even use the word love so casually.

"I did deceive you tonight, Jessie, and in the most personal way, but I would never lie about love to avoid having my ass chewed out." Come to think of it, he couldn't remember anyone ever arguing with him before--besides his father or Carolyn. Most people were too busy kissing his ass instead.

"At least one part of your statement is true--you did deceive me. Do you have any idea how hard it was for me to be open enough with someone and think about what I wanted for me for a change?" She'd kept her emotions so guarded for the last few years; she barely even knew who she was anymore.

"I don't like being called a liar, Jessie, so I'm only going to say this once. I'm sorry I deceived you, and I'll take the blame for that part." He was beginning to get angry himself and knew that if she didn't want to see what an alpha male he could really be, she'd be smart to not test him on his declaration of love again.

She took a few steps back, overwhelmed at the fire that filled his gaze. He wasn't denying he'd been wrong about the dungeon charade, but he was telling her he meant what he said about being in love with her. Refusing to back down, she still took his words to heart. "Fine, for now we'll bypass the whole love con-fession." Which she still felt was a lie, but she wasn't about to call him again on that yet. "Why would you step into the role when Carolyn had to have made it obvious I was trying to find someone new?"

"Because the thought of you playing with someone else that way pissed me off, and I wanted it to be me instead." He wasn't going to deny he was a jealous man. If she wanted to be angry about that, then that at least was fair.

She could only stare at him. "So you do this with all your submissive's?" *Talk about control issues,* she thought, shaking her head.

He chuckled at her conclusion. "No. Just one raven-haired beauty who won't leave my dreams long enough to allow me to focus on anyone or anything else."

How could she argue with that? She thought as her mouth hung open. Was it even possible that this gorgeous hunk of man thought about her as much as she did him? She wanted again to believe, but it just couldn't be true. Then again, what did he have to gain from continuously lying to her?

Still, she wasn't convinced he wasn't just toying with her. It just didn't make sense that he could want her as desperately as she wanted him. "Chase," she said finally, "if you're just looking for someone to play around with, you don't need to keep coming up with all these lies. Obviously I want you. Even if I know it's going to break my heart when you walk away."

"So you do still want me?" He hadn't forgotten she'd just called him a liar again, but he wanted to know how she felt before he reacted to that.

"You'd have to be blind not to know how appealing I find you." She was going to regret being so honest with him, but she was tired of the game he was playing. The dungeon tonight proved she still wanted to experience more, and even if she knew her heart was going to be dragged through the mud, she couldn't deny it was him she wanted to play with.

"I just want to be sure I understand what you are saying, Jessie. You want to continue playing with me, and you'll agree not to go out and try to find someone else to train you?"

She knew if she agreed to be his, things were about to get intense. But she couldn't deny that was what she wanted. "Yes, Chase, as much as I'm sure it strokes your ego, I haven't really thought about anyone else since I met you. If you want to train me, I won't look for anyone else." God, she was such an idiot. Giving him the power to break her heart was singlehandedly the most stupid idea she'd ever had.

"Tell me you belong to me, Jessie." He moved close until they were standing only inches apart. "Tell me you want only me as your master." His eyes probed hers as he waited impatiently for her answer. It was the most important question he'd ever asked a woman in his life.

She hated herself for being so weak, but she couldn't deny how much she wanted to be his. Even if he decided later on that this was all a game to him and walked away, she wanted this time. God, how she wanted him--to feel the sensations only he could give, and enjoy the tenderness she knew he was capable of. "Yes, damn you, I belong to you."

He'd held his breath as he waited for her answer and when she gave it, he released it forcefully. "Get in your car and follow me home." It wasn't a request. There were several things they needed to discuss, and he wasn't about to do it in a public place. He saw the hesitancy in her eyes, and realized how abruptly he'd spoken. "Come home, Jessie. I don't want to finish this conversation here." She would never be hesitant with him again, he declared mentally as her feet finally moved to her car.

Jessie drove back to his house with a million thoughts moving through her mind. She'd just agreed to belong to him--only him-- and there was no denying where that would lead. The thought of being in his bed, or even in his dungeon, didn't frighten her at all-- she knew how capable he was of drawing out her sexuality. What scared the living hell out of her was giving him her heart. If he decided to walk away, that would hurt more than any physical act.

Neither of them talked as they finally arrived at his place in separate cars. He led her straight up to his bedroom and she trembled as he finally turned to look into her eyes. The thought of belonging to him was overwhelming and she had no idea just what she meant to him. To her, it meant she'd give everything she had to please him.

"Undress." He spoke calmly, attempting to not scare the shit out of her by revealing how much he wanted her.

She didn't even hesitate to strip off her clothes, fueled by the look of desire in his eyes as each piece found the floor. There was something so sexy about being commanded to do his bidding.

His eyes roamed over her incredible body, not missing one delicious inch of the perfection before him. "Get in bed and wait for me, Jessie girl." Keeping his voice from demanding her compliance was almost impossible, and he noted how she quickly walked over to the bed and rested back on the pillows. He was pleased at how easily she allowed him to guide her. He quickly undressed and joined her.

Lying beside her, he lifted up on one arm and glanced deeply into her eyes. "Are you sure this is what you want, Jessie Girl? And before you answer, let me be perfectly clear. I won't take anything less than every ounce of passion you have to give, and I'll demand things of your body that you never even thought possible before. So tell me, Jessie, do you still want to be mine?" If she said no, he was going to have a seriously hard time letting her leave.

She bit her lip and nodded, not even sure she could speak at the moment. The intensity in his dark blue eyes told her she would be surrendering everything to him, and oddly enough, she wanted nothing less than to be completely his. "Say the words, Jessie girl. I don't want there ever to be any doubt about what you're agreeing to."

"I want to be yours completely, Chase," she managed to whisper, even though the words caught in her throat, making her sound less confident than she truly was about giving herself over to him. He was the most intimidating male she'd ever met, even though she knew he was also capable of incredible compassion.

He smiled warmly at her words before moving between her thighs. The look in her eyes told him much more than her hesitant words. Resting his lower body against hers, he allowed her to feel just how much he desired her. "Jessie girl, you have no idea of the things I'm going to do to you." Lowering his head, he kissed her passionately.

Returning his kiss, she was sure she didn't know, but with his hard shaft rubbing against her sensitive folds, she was definitely willing to find out. Wrapping her arms around his neck, she held him tightly and arched her hips up to rub against him desperately.

Allowing her tempting little body free will for a few more moments, he knew if he didn't control her, he was going to lose what little self control he had left. He quickly found the cuffs attached to the bed and had her arms secured in seconds. "After I love you, Jessie girl, I'm going to punish you for calling me a liar." He smirked and moved himself down the bed to put his head between her thighs.

His unveiled threat sent a tremble of anticipation through her body, but she had little time to think about it as his tongue found her core and brought her to the brink of ecstasy. Over and over, he held her on the edge and pulled away until she was ready to scream in frustration. He knew this game well, obviously, and played her body with perfection.

The sight of her tiny form writhing in pleasure demanded he fulfill his own needs, but he wasn't ready for her to find nirvana just yet. Rolling over to the bedside table, he slid a condom on within seconds. Moving back between her thighs, his cock rested at the entrance of her core. He pushed in slightly, and then recoiled, enjoying the look of longing on her face. "I could tease you like this all night, Jessie." Again, he gave a slight thrust and retreated, not sure if he was killing her or himself.

"Chase, please," she demanded, arching up as he pulled away again. This was the ultimate torture-- knowing what pleasure he could give with his body and being denied.

The look in her eyes and the soft whimper escaping her lips was enough, he decided as he filled her completely with one long thrust. He enjoyed the sensation of feeling like he'd finally come home for a few moments before his body took over. With each delicious thrust, her body clung to him like a second skin and he almost hated pulling away again. She was made to love him like this, he thought as he increased his power and took her with a reckless abandon that left them both gasping for air when release came.

Shaking his head, he chuckled loudly. "Jessie girl, do you have any idea how good you make me feel?" Keeping his body weight on his upper arms, he lowered his face to brush her lips with his.

She had an inclination, since her legs were pretty much like jelly as she basked in the aftermath, feeling incredible. "I hope as good as you make me feel," she whispered. Glancing up into his beautiful eyes, she smiled shyly.

She was amazed at how incredible being with him was. If other people were this lucky in finding the perfect lover, she couldn't understand why they didn't spend their entire lives wrapped in that lover's arms. *Who needed material things when there was this,* she thought with a small laugh.

He rolled out of bed and slid on his underwear, pleased by the sound of her laughter. "I want you to know how much you please me, Jessie girl." He smiled at her.

"You pleased me, too." She glanced up at him expectantly, wondering why he was now wearing underwear again.

"That's my job." He winked, and sat down on the edge of the bed. Patting the place beside him, he waited until she was sitting next to him. "My other job is to make sure you know that when I tell you something, you believe it."

His tone had deepened, and for reasons she didn't understand, it made her heart race nervously. "I'm not sure I understand," she said, nibbling on her lip.

He wrapped his arm around her shoulder, pulling her against him as he looked down into her confused eyes. Still smiling reassuringly, he explained, "I told you I loved you tonight. You threw that back in my face, assuming I was lying." He saw the fear she couldn't hide, and lowered his lips to her cheek to place a chaste kiss there. "I would never lie about loving you."

She trembled nervously and wasn't sure that she liked how guilty his statement made her feel. "How could I believe someone like you could really love me?" Lowering her eyes, the earlier contentment from their passionate lovemaking dissipated.

Shaking his head at her lack of confidence, he sighed. "Jessie girl, I don't know whether I should pull you over my lap and spank you, or hug you until you realize how incredible you are." Pulling her into his arms he decided to start with the latter. "You are perfection to me Jessie girl. I refused to let you believe anything else." Lifting her chin, he stared down into her eyes. "Maybe I'll do both," referring back to hugging or spanking her, he lowered his lips to hers and kissed her passionately.

Both? Her mind tried to keep up with his words, but his kiss was enough to take her breath away.

When her arms wrapped around his neck, he knew she wasn't truly hearing him. He pulled back and smiled into her heated gaze. "Definitely, both," he chuckled and patted his lap.

She looked up at him in confusion. *He's not really going to spank me,* her mind finally caught up with what he'd said.

"Over my knee Jessie girl," patting his lap again, he waited patiently for her to move.

With awkward movements, she slid off the bed, and rested over his lap. A part of her mind told her to be afraid, but all she really felt was anticipation. She knew instinctively he wouldn't hurt her. With that brazen thought she wiggled her butt.

Chuckling at her bravado, he rested his hand on her exquisite ass. "The things I could do with these lovely twin mounds." Kneading the firm flesh for a few moments, he then allowed his hand to fall down with a little force.

Tensing at the slight sting, she was shocked to realize it turned her on. As his hand fell again on the opposite cheek, she moaned. Rotating her hips, she felt her core drench as his hand continued to reign down on her tender flesh with building intensity.

The sight of her beautiful ass tinged with a slight pink color had him hard instantly. Massaging tenderly, he thought of ways to please her in this position. "You have no idea what I want to do this delectable ass, Jessie girl." Sliding his hand around to her core, two fingers plunged deep.

"Chase!" God, there was something so erotic about being draped over his knee this way. She almost found release.

Sliding his fingers from her silken heat, his hand landed firmly on her ass again. "This is mine, Jessie girl, say it."

His fingers moved back to her core and he stroked slowly across the hardened nub of her clit.

"It's yours." She whimpered the words as his fingers left her aching as they pulled away again.

Moving back to reign down small slaps against her ass again, he allowed his thumb to push against the bud of her other chamber. "This is mine too. Soon I'm claiming it. Will you deny it?"

Shaking her head no, the sensations he was racking on her body refused to allow her to deny him anything. "No, anything you want."

Smiling at her words he slowly pushed his thumb inside. Pleased that she didn't tense against the invasion, he slowly rode her with the digit as his forefinger slid over her clit. "There will be no part of your body that I won't claim, Jessie girl," he warned. The intensity in his voice showed he was serious.

Her body tensed as he continued to ride her with her fingers, on the edge of paradise. "I need you to claim me," she sobbed. *The man's fingers are magical*, she thought as he held her on the precipice, then stilled.

Pulling his fingers away slowly, he showered her ass with a few more playful slaps. Then he pulled her up to sit in his lap. "There's one other part that will belong to me, Jessie girl. Do you know what that is?" Staring intently into her eyes he smiled.

"I have no idea." *What other part could he want?*

Resting his hand against her breast, over her heart, he raised a brow. "Your heart, Jessie girl. In return I give you mine." At the look of doubt that crossed her face, his expression hardened. "You won't doubt that." He demanded, his hand moving under her chin to hold it firmly. "Do you think I'm a stupid man?"

"Of course not, you're one of the smartest men I know." Wiggling on his lap, she attempted to force away the ache his earlier touch had left.

Smiling at her movement, he released the grip on her chin, and caressed her cheek. "Then trust me when I say I love you Jessie girl. I am intelligent enough to know when I'm holding the most precious thing in my life in my lap at this moment."

The look of possession and love that filled his eyes left her with no doubt that his words were true. "I love you too, Chase." Her eyes filled with tears as she confessed the truth. She was amazed. This beautiful, strong man loved her.

Standing with her in his arms, he walked into the bathroom. "I'm never letting you leave me again, Jessie girl." He warned as they stepped under the steaming water he'd started in the shower.

He washed her body, seeming to worship her with his hands. Leaning in to his touch, she felt her heart soar with his words. "What if you grow bored with me?" There was still that niggling doubt at the back of her mind that she didn't deserve him.

Pulling her against his body, he allowed her to feel how much he desired her. "Does this feel like I could ever get bored with you?" He chuckled and lifted her leg to wrap around his waist. Rubbing his cock against the silkiness of her core, he teased. "We are going to explore every ounce of desire your body has to offer, and then go beyond even that."

Moaning softly as her body responded, she pushed against him. "So we're going to spend all our free time in the bedroom?" Nothing sounded sweeter at that moment, she thought. Reaching her hand down, she grasped him in her hand and began stroking in slow, even motions.

"My dungeon, my bedroom, on top of a mountain," growling deeply, his body demanded release as her hand squeezed. Dislodging her hand, he walked her backward until she was against the back of the shower stall. Lifting her up, she wrapped her legs around his waist and he drove in deeply.

Impaled on his impressive length, she cried out with each thrust. His hand wrapped in her hair, and he pulled until her head arched back. Never missing a stroke, he lowered his face to nuzzle her neck, as he drove deeply and retreated. "Mine, Jessie girl. Don't you dare forget it!"

How could she want to belong to anyone else, she thought. She screamed out as her body found paradise, her hands gripping his shoulders at the force of her release.

Perfection, he thought as his cock was gripped and released as she came. That was all it took, he couldn't hold back. With a deep growl, he filled her. It took several moments for him to realize he'd forgotten a condom, and he shook his head at his forgetfulness. "How do you feel about kids?" In all his years he'd never been so irresponsible, the things this beautiful woman did to him!

He untangled their bodies, and she looked at him perplexed. "I like kids." She had no idea why he chose this moment to bring it up.

Pulling her back under the water, he rinsed her off, hoping she wasn't going to be angry. "I forgot to use a condom."

He looked so horrified, she couldn't help but giggle. "I wouldn't mind having your child." Saying the words, she knew they were true. She really did like kids. The thought of ever meeting a man she'd be willing to have them with had been the problem.

"You should be kicking my ass right now." He shook his head, stepped out of the shower, and retrieved towels. He dried her off first, and then took care of his own needs. "I won't be that irresponsible again, Jessie girl, you have my word." *If she wasn't pregnant now.* He knew he was physically healthy. He'd always used condoms in the past, and had a yearly check up.

"I think it takes two, Chase," she grinned. Walking over, she lifted up on her tiptoes to kiss his cheek. "I got on the pill after our first night together." The thought of having his child wasn't abhorrent though.

Sighing in relief, he smiled. "I think kids in the future would be nice. As long as they're planned." Pulling her into arms, he hugged her tightly. "Let's get back in bed." Without giving her time to accept or decline, he lifted her into his arms.

Laughing, snuggled back in his arms in bed again, she gave a content sigh. "I love you." She wanted to keep saying those words over and over.

"I love you, Jessie girl." He spent the rest of the evening showing her without words.

CHAPTER NINETEEN

Jessie Girl

The last six months had been more incredible than any dream she'd ever had. She'd moved in with Chase last month and doing so had bonded them even more. Her mind had been opened to a world of incredible pleasures, things that would have seemed overwhelming before he'd walked into her life. Happiness couldn't even describe how loved and cherished she felt with her alpha male.

The book club meeting tonight was something she wasn't really looking forward too. Not because she didn't love her friends, but because she had her own love story to live and it was hard to leave him, if only for a night. Carolyn had become almost as dear to her as Amanda, since they played in the same world. It hadn't taken long to realize the small deception she'd taken part in by sending Chase to her that night in the dungeon had turned into a priceless gift she would never be able to repay.

The woman who walked into the meeting tonight was so different from the girl she had once been, she thought. Her beautiful master had given her confidence and helped her discover the strong, powerful woman who had been hiding behind the wallflower. No longer did she feel uncomfortable with her body. Being put on a pedestal by her lover had the most amazing effect on her self-esteem. There was no doubt in her mind that Chase loved everything about her.

Tonight she was dressed to accentuate her body's features. Chase had taught her that dressing her body in flattering ways encouraged the world to see a confident woman who never felt out of place. The group of women she'd previously felt awkward around due to her lack of fashion sense now asked her where she purchased her clothing.

Sitting down with the group tonight, she glanced around with an air of confidence that came from knowing she was just as worthy as every other woman in that room. Liberating was how she explained her new life with Chase. He encouraged her to become a woman who knew who she was and what she required in life.

"Ladies, I know we were supposed to discuss the new book we added to our list last week, but I have a special surprise for you tonight." Carolyn smiled as she spoke.

Jessie glanced around at the other ladies then at Carolyn. She was curious about what could be more important than discussing the new book. It was actually one of her favorite new authors, so she hoped whatever Carolyn had planned would prove to be entertaining.

"If you would, follow me downstairs." Seemingly unable to contain her glee, Carolyn laughed warmly.

Jessie stood and glanced at Amanda, then shrugged. Amanda's expression appeared as confused as her own. They followed Carolyn downstairs and collective gasps filled the room as they noticed the band set-up. She doubted her shock wasn't mirrored on the faces of the other ladies when they saw the lead singer. He was a pop idol icon from the eighties.

The song was one she knew well since Chase had a huge love of 1980's music and he'd dedicated that song to her one night while they were dancing. She was confounded. It seemed a little too coincidental that a band playing their song, just happened to be in Carolyn's basement. Her heart began to race.

At the end of the song, all the lights in the room dimmed for a brief moment. When they came back up seconds later, Chase was standing where the singer had been, holding a microphone. Jessie felt her heart flutter into her stomach as he gave that smile that always left her a little short of breath.

"Jessie girl, these last six months with you have been the greatest of my life. I know there will never be another woman who fills my heart the way you do. Would you do me the honor of becoming my wife?" He placed the microphone in the stand and walked the few feet over to join her before kneeling down. Holding up a beautiful solitaire diamond in a red velvet box, he looked up at her, his eyes filled with love.

Staring down into the most beautiful blue eyes she'd ever seen, tears of happiness slid down her cheeks. Nodding, too emotional to speak the words, she held out her trembling hand.

Sliding the ring on her finger, he looked up and smiled like a man who had just been given the greatest gift in the world. *She would be his Jessie girl for all time.* "I promise to spend the rest of my life making you happy."

Kneeling with him, she wrapped her arms around his neck and hugged him as tightly as her small frame would allow. "I love you, Chase." Those words didn't even begin to express the emotion she had for this proud, gorgeous man. He'd given her so much. A lifetime wasn't even a sliver of the amount of time she needed to show how deeply she loved him.

The sound of laughter and clapping filled their ears as his lips found hers. They ignored the crowd. For that brief moment, it was just the two of them. He might be an alpha male, but his control vanished at the thought of knowing she was truly his now forever. "I'll never let you go, Jessie girl," he whispered.

"I would find you if you did," she said, laughing as they stood up together. She knew this moment in time would be engraved in her mind when she was telling their grandchildren about how he proposed.

The celebration of their engagement went on for hours. By the time the band had finally called it a night, both of them were looking forward to a little alone time. When Carolyn finally told the group she needed to call it a night, Chase and Jessie could only smile at each other, knowing finally they could leave without hurting anyone's feelings.

Jessie hugged Carolyn as they made their way to the front door. "Thank you for everything, Carolyn. This has been the most magical night of my life." That didn't even begin to express how appreciative she was for all this woman had done for her.

Hugging her back, Carolyn smiled in happiness. "I guess you never really know what goes on behind the scenes at a romance book club." She laughed deeply. "I know you'll have a wonderful life together, Jessie." She hugged Chase as he appeared with their jackets. "Take care of her, Chase." Winking, she watched them walk out the door.

CHAPTER TWENTY

Epilogue

Sitting down at her computer, Jessie smiled at the finished rough draft manuscript filling the screen. Fifteen years ago she married the most wonderful man, and her life had been so full of great memories. Eventually she decided to write them all down.

Chase had given his blessing on the project, and even agreed to personally help her research if there were things she'd forgotten. Some interesting nights came from their so-called research. Glancing over at the still handsome man across the room in bed, she smiled lovingly.

She'd taken over Amanda's fathers company when he passed away three years ago, so the writing was just a part-time hobby. Amanda was enjoying her inheritance and had recently called from Paris telling her how much she enjoyed travelling now that she wasn't tied to a company she never wanted.

Chase had signed over Sensation's fully to Carolyn, and it was flourishing well under her ownership. His own business was doing even better than he'd considered possible, so they both had full lives outside of their marriage.

Their twins were almost teenagers now, and even though it was hard working away from home, they were doing well with the arrangement. Life had turned out just the way she'd always dreamed.

Saving the document to her hard drive, she couldn't wait to hear what the publisher thought. Romance Book Club, it seemed a fitting title to a romance that encompassed everything she was. Walking back to the bed, she slid in quietly beside Chase.

BOOK CLUB GROUP GUIDE

ROMANCE
BOOK CLUB

Michelle Hughes

Tears of Crimson

**To discover more about Michelle Hughes visit
www.tearsofcrimson.com**

INTRODUCTION

Jessie discovers there's more to reality than what you read in the pages of a romance book when her book reader's club decides to take their research into the real world of BDSM. Being a self-titled recluse does nothing to prepare her for the sensual world she's exposed to at the dungeon club, Sensations. Closing her heart off for years after her long term boyfriend admits his homosexuality; she discovers a world of temptations with the offer to explore them all thanks to club owner, Chase Davenport. Chase fits none of the stereotypes for the egotistical alpha males they've read about in the romance novels, and if she takes the chance her own perceptions of self may soon become something she can soon leave in the past as well.

QUESTIONS FOR DISCUSSION

1. Romance Book Club's back theme is about women who enjoy meeting to discuss their love of great romance novels. Would your reading club ever take the research of a book as far as they did? How do you think the members in your book club would react if they walked into a real life BDSM dungeon?

2. As avid readers, what fantasies have you thought of exploring thanks to the pages in a book? Do you think the
reality would be as exciting as the novel?

3. In Romance Book Club the woman are all professionals in one capacity or another. Do you think that a

status of a person makes a difference when it comes to how they would approach a BDSM Relationship?

4. Did you discover anything about BDSM in this book that changed your perception of the lifestyle? If so what were some of those things, and what did you think before?

5. Romance Book Club stayed away from the egotistical alpha male type hero in this book. We wanted to show a softer side instead of what the majority of books are portraying now. Was it hard to accept that a man could be dominant without having an emotional hang up from the past? What about the confidence Jessie discovered thanks to his teaching, was that something you'd considered possible in this type of relationship?

6. BDSM is no longer a taboo discussion for the most part, due to the mainstream media's recent fascination. What books other than Romance Book Club have you discovered that recently interested you about this once secretive topic of conversation?

7. Chase is considerably one of the most respectful men you could hope to meet in today's society. After getting to know him in the book do you think he secretly embraced the BDSM lifestyle at first to show his independence from his father's conservative values?

We hope you enjoyed walking behind the scenes of a Romance Book Club. There are so many great groups that share a love of reading, and we hope you'll take the time to visit the ones in your local neighborhood or join us online for ours. We love discussing romance at http://www.facebook.com/TOCRB

16472794R00149

Printed in Great Britain
by Amazon